FAUX BEAU'S BABY SURPRISE

CALLIE STEVENS

1

DANA

The house is quiet. I don't like it.

My childhood home has always been filled with noise. I mean, five girls will do that. Someone always has something going on.

Except, not lately, I guess, with everyone slowly moving on and moving out.

Can you suffer from empty-nest syndrome when you're not even a mom?

God, life was simple once, wasn't it? Now? Nor so much.

I tighten my hands around my cup of coffee, the warmth seeping through my palms and into my body.

Two arms loop around my waist. Kira tucks her chin on my shoulder. "Morning, sis."

I giggle and snuggle with my sister. "Hi, honey. You just rolled out of bed, huh?"

"I was at the office late working on a bug," Kira grumbles and then trudges over to the coffee pot. Her brown hair is lumpy and unbrushed and the lenses of her glasses could use buffing.

"You're working too hard," I say as kindly as I can, though I'm starting to get worried. Ever since management at Kira's company began to change hands, she's been working overtime.

Kira shrugs. "It's not like I have anything else to do."

Yeah, me either. Only, my job doesn't afford me the luxury of overtime, unless I took on a couple more clients. Still, though, would be nice not to have to think about my own problems.

"Besides, Orlie gave me the day off," Kira says with a yawn.

"Kira. It's Saturday."

She stops in her tracks and then mutters, "Damn, that jackass."

"Dana! What a surprise!" Dad announces as he comes into the kitchen.

I frown. "It's the second Saturday of the month."

"I suppose it is," he says with a cheery grin, tightening his striped necktie.

"We usually all get together for breakfast on this day," I say.

Dad chuckles. "Well, at least you two keep up with tradition."

I bristle. "Is no one else coming?"

"I thought we'd kind of done away with the second Saturday breakfast thing," Kira says uneasily.

My heart sinks. "Amy's not home?"

"That's her new default," Kira says.

I see Dad wince as he pours himself a cup of coffee. "I wouldn't say default..."

"Daddy, she's engaged. It's only a matter of time before she moves out," Kira says with a smile. "Right, Dana?"

I blink. I guess I hadn't realized that our silly monthly tradition had petered out.

Sure, since Harley had Tana, she'd been more sparing in her attendance. And when Gillian and Axel got together, I guess she had started dedicating more time to being with him. That left just Kira, Amy, and me.

And now Amy...

"You girls want pancakes?" Dad asks, opening one of the cabinets for a box of Bisquick.

"Only if they're chocolate chip," Kira says.

"This is how I know you're my daughter," he says, wrapping an arm around her and giving her a side hug. "What about you, Dana?"

I look down at the steam coming out of my coffee, which is less and less as it cools. "Huh?"

Dad eyes me for a second. "Chocolate chip for Kira, blueberry for Dana."

I try to smile. "Thanks."

Kira comes to sit at the island with me, one of her eyebrows cocked upward as if to ask, *Are you okay?*

I nod.

She knows I'm lying. But she doesn't push it. That's the Kira way. Whereas I tease everyone's feelings out of them so they won't keep them bottled up, Kira waits for people to open themselves up to her. Two sides of the same coin.

"And then there were two, huh?" Dad calls out as he pours milk into a bowl of Bisquick.

"I could text Amy," Kira says. "She'd come over."

"Oh, no, no. Don't do that." Dad props the bowl on his hip and stirs it like he's a perfect fifties housewife. "You girls are all growing up. That's the way it should be," he says with a wistful smile.

I smile back. Dad knows that, eventually, he'll be left all

alone in the big house. Must be a scary thought. I'm scared for him too. "Maybe I should move back in," I say as casually as I can. After all, it's not like I've got anyone waiting at home for me.

Kira does a doubletake. "What?!"

"No!" Dad says simultaneously.

I cross my arms over my chest. "Damn, tell me how you *really* feel."

"I mean, we'd love to have you, Dana. If that's what you need," Dad starts explaining. "But you've got your own life."

I sigh. "Do I, though?"

"Of course you do!" he replies. "You've got the practice and...and..."

I narrow my eyes. He can't even name a second thing. Yeah, I'm officially pathetic.

"You've got Drew," Kira says with a sly smile.

"Why are you saying it like that?" I ask. We've had this interaction at least four dozen times at this point.

Kira scoffs. "Don't act like–"

"Nothing is happening," I hiss. "Drop it."

Drew and I have been friends for a few years now. He used to be my client in grief counseling and then, when he felt he'd reached closure after his mother's death, he left... then came back a week later with an extra ticket to a Dodgers game that he then invited me to. As a long-suffering baseball fan, how could I refuse?

It was not a date and has never and will never be romantic.

Even if I want it to be.

"Dana, it's sweet of you to offer, but you've already done so much for our family. You're our rock. I couldn't ask you to do any more than you already have," Dad explains, folding a bag of chocolate chips into the batter.

I guess I do have that to be proud of. I'm a good big sister and daughter. A great one.

Their rock, as dad says. I just wish that someday I find my own rock too.

"I don't like the idea of you being here all alone," I say.

Kira gapes. "Hey! What am I, chopped liver?"

"I just mean *eventually*. Once you move out."

Kira rolls her eyes. "As long as I'm working for Orlie Wynters, there will be no social life to speak of. Living at home is just fine for me."

My eyes meet Dad's and he smiles, pointing his spatula at Kira. "See? I have Kira."

I shake my head. "We need to get you a girlfriend, Dad."

He flushes. "A girlfr–No, no. I'm much too old for that."

"A lady friend, then," Kira adds, elbowing me. We both giggle.

"Girls–"

"Dad, we're teasing," I interrupt him. *Kind of.* Dad hasn't been with anyone, as far as I know, since Mom left. That was over ten years ago now. "Although, I did see you getting kind of cozy with Victoria at–"

Dad gasps. "Victoria?! No. That's my best friend's sister."

"Are you talking about the best friend who is literally married to your daughter? *That* best friend?" Kira retorts.

Dad huffs, unable to find his next sentence for several moments before firmly saying, "I don't get cozy with anyone." Then, he turns his back to us to start working on the griddle, effectively ending the conversation.

Kira and I try not to laugh.

"WHAT DO PEOPLE WEAR IN MALDIVES?" Kira asks as we wade through the racks at Fred Segal.

"I think there's a difference between what people wear in Maldives and what people at a *resort* wear in Maldives," I say dryly.

Gillian and Axel are getting married at the end of the month. I definitely didn't expect a destination wedding from them, but I guess I have to thank Hunter Ricks, Amy's hotel magnate beau and Dad's next-door neighbor, for offering Gillian and Axel full run of Ricks Maldives from Christmas to New Year's.

Needless to say, this is going to be the event of a lifetime.

However, I don't have a wardrobe suitable for a resort.

I take a floral caftan off the rack. We both immediately grimace.

"This isn't going well, is it?" Kira murmurs.

I laugh. "Please, we just started."

"You know I hate shopping."

I glance at her over my shoulder as I start to push pieces down a rack. Moments like these make me feel like a mom. Dragging a kid around a store for new school clothes. Except it's my sister and we're shopping for a luxury resort. Same, but different. "Maybe we should start with bathing suits."

"I have a bathing suit," Kira replies.

"You have a speedo one piece that you use for exercise. You're not wearing that on a beach in Maldives."

Kira snorts. "I'll do whatever I like."

"Don't be difficult."

"I'm not."

Over the chasm of a rack of billowy palazzo pants, we glare at each other. I swear to god, the next child I deal with better be my own.

Who am I kidding, though? That's not going to happen for...well, hopefully not *a million* years, but...not any time soon either. Unfortunately.

"Tell you what. I'll give you ten minutes to find a bathing suit, an outfit for the rehearsal dinner, and a New Year's Eve dress. Then we can go."

Kira's dark brown eyes sparkle. "You know I can't resist a challenge."

I laugh. "Yeah, I know." I pull out my phone and start to set a timer. I can go shopping on my own time, linger in the racks until I find the perfect outfits when I don't have my little sister clamoring around saying she's bored. "Ready, set, go!"

Kira starts to scramble around Fred Segal like a bat out of hell. It's funny to watch how the salespeople stare at her, wide-eyed and confused that anyone would dare come to their store and not languish in it with a credit card in their outstretched hand.

I see her pull out a basic black bathing suit and tsk her. "Uh-uh-uh. Has to be colorful!"

"You didn't say *that*!" she snaps.

"Or a bikini," I grin.

Of course I want my sister to feel comfortable, but I don't want her to regret not going full hog when pictures from the wedding come back and she decided to fade into the back like she always tries to with her hair in a simple ponytail and basic blacks.

While Kira curses me under her breath, my phone goes off. She gasps. "That was not ten minutes!"

"Relax, I'm getting a call." I peer down at the name.

"Who is it?"

I hesitate. "It's Drew."

"Ooooh. It's *Drew*," Kira grins and waggles her eyebrows.

"Don't make that face," I say and stare at the phone as it vibrates in my hand.

"Well... answer it!" Kira encourages. "Answer it, answer–"

"I will!"

Drew calling is not an event. We chat on the phone all the time just to touch base. He's just being nice.

However, I can't help my heart from racing when I answer the phone.

2

DREW

"Hello?"

Even when her voice is all garbled on the phone, I feel my face get hot. "What are you doing for lunch today?"

"Hi, Drew."

I roll my eyes and smile to myself. "Hi, *Dana.*"

"Were you raised in a barn or did you never learn you need to *greet* people when you call them on the phone?"

I lean on the wall outside the conference room and smile to myself. "You know, this never came up in counseling, but I was indeed raised in a–"

Before I can even finish my sentence, Dana laughs. A big peel of laughter. God, it's like music to my ears every time. "You're an idiot," she says as her laugh peters out.

Reese, my boss, pokes his head out of the workshop. "Hey, Drew, we're ready for you."

"One sec," I mouth quickly. Everyone's in the office today, on a Saturday, for my presentation. Don't want to keep them waiting.

But Dana's more important.

"Anyway, you were saying?"

"Yes, lunch. Meet me for lunch."

Dana sighs, "I'm out with Kira."

My heart sinks just a tad. Only a tad. I love the whole Solace family. More than that, I love how much Dana loves her family. I'm out here on my own. It's nice to be a part of their fold. I'd be lying, though, if I didn't say I was looking forward to potentially some one on one time with Dana. "Well, bring her. The more, the merrier."

"You sure?" she asks, her voice bright.

"Of course! Just tell her to be nice to me."

"Oh, she's always nice."

Harley might be the sassiest Solace girl, but Kira's got this scathing wit that seems to come out of nowhere. She's quiet and a bit mousey, then *boom*. She reads you for filth. "Yeah, so nice that she told me one time that my haircut made me look like Jeff Bezos."

"You have to admit, it *was* a bad haircut."

"Dana. Jeff Bezos is bald," I reply.

I hear Kira say something on the other end and the two girls both laugh.

"I hear you talking about me!"

"She says he wasn't always bald."

I try to restrain my smile. "Do you want me to take you two out to lunch or not?"

"Yes! Yes, please. Say sorry, Kira."

Dana and Kira bicker for a moment before I hear Kira say, "Fine. Sorry. I won't say anything about your hair ever again."

"Or lack thereof," I reply.

Kira laughs wildly and then Dana gets back on the phone. "Where and when?"

"What are you feeling?" I ask.

"Drew–" Reed pokes his head out again, jerking his head back into the room. "We're. Ready. For. You!"

I ignore him in lieu of Dana's answer. "Tacos."

"Great. Rietta's at one. Sound good?"

"Perfect."

Yes. Perfect.

We exchange goodbyes; when I hang up, I try not to stand there and swoon too long. I've got a presentation to do.

"Sorry, had to take a phone call!" I announce as I walk into the workshop. "I know you're all on the edge of your seats, so–" I grin and scan the crowd of my peers. When you think of engineers, I bet you imagine people who are nerdy and strait-laced. Here, though, at Filston Technology, we're an eclectic bunch of outsiders with piercings, tattoos, and no dress code to speak of. We're in it for the love of the game, not the money.

Although, it helps that the money is good.

"Let me introduce to you an engine that is not just carbon neutral, not just carbon zero, but *carbon negative.* I introduce to you the world's first truly green vehicle engine," I explain before tapping on my computer to pull up the schematics. "The first engine to run fully and completely on carbon dioxide."

Reese leans back in his seat and smiles. "Well, I'll be damned. I'd say that's worth waiting for."

I smile. "That's an understatement."

My presentation is a success. Everyone is humming with excitement by the end, fielding questions, wondering about the timeline. By no means is this engine going to come together quickly. But if I can swing it...I'll change the face of automotive technology. We can actually do something good for the environment rather than just trying to offset the harm we've already done.

If only my mother could see me now. She'd be so proud of me.

Although, I often worry that she might not be as proud as I'd hope.

Don't get me wrong, my mom was the most loving creature on the face of the earth. She put up with so much shit she didn't deserve and didn't even get a full life before the cancer took her.

After the presentation, I head out to Rietta's. I should be celebrating my accomplishment, but I'm still thinking about my mom. And one of our final conversations.

Toward the end, she was in hospice. It wasn't an "If" she'd go but a "when". All I cared about was that she was comfortable and attended to. But it was a lot for me to handle. I was so young. At least I felt so much younger than I am now.

I wasn't the best type of guy when I was in my twenties. What guy is? I could have been better to her.

But anyway, we were watching an episode of *Full House* which was her favorite. I always got the sense she wished she'd had gotten a chance to have more children or that we had more family nearby. Instead, though, it was just me and her.

In the middle of the episode, she turned to me, grabbed my hand with the little bit of strength she had left and smiled. Her smiles had started to look...maniacal. Her face had gotten so gaunt with the illness, hair looking like straw, eyes losing their luster. She didn't look like my mom anymore. However, in moments, she was there as her full, healthy self. This was one of them. "I want that for you, Drew."

"What?" I asked with a half-smile, wondering if she was starting to lose it.

"A family. A big one. Do you want that, baby?"

At the time, I was one of those young guys who saw children screaming in public and rolled my eyes. As I've gotten older, that feeling has changed. Especially being close to the Solaces. I've watched Stella grow up and witnessed Harley become a mother. I understand now that children and family are two of the most precious things.

Especially since I don't have one of my own to speak of.

"Yeah, Mom," I answered. I did everything I could to make her happy. "One day."

She squeezed my hand. "Good. You'll make a good husband. A good father. I know you will."

I think of that conversation often. Because, though I want to be a husband and a father now, I'm not sure I *would* be good at it. I want to be worthy and deserving of a woman's love, a love so powerful she's willing to join our bodies together to create something so...unbelievably precious.

Is it crazy that I see that with Dana sometimes? I've had feelings for her for two years now. It started before I stopped going to counseling. In fact, it's partly why I stopped. I couldn't focus anymore on my own grief. Every session was just her dazzling smile, plaintive expression, the way her curls bobbled as she took notes.

I've watched her watch three of her sisters fall in love and build lives with other people. Perhaps Dana might be ready to see me that way?

I've been driving for a while now on autopilot. I blink and scan my surroundings as I come to a stoplight. That could have been bad.

My phone buzzes in its holder on the dashboard. I grab

it and quickly check the text that's just come in, hoping I can beat the light.

It's from Kira.

You're welcome.

What?

I scroll up to see if there's another text, but there isn't. That's all there is. All she wrote. *You're welcome.*

Maybe she didn't mean to text me. Regardless, I tap off a message fast.

For what?

I stare at the phone, waiting for a reply.

The blare of a horn shoots into my ears. I drop the phone and it clatters right in the slot between my seat and the center console. "Shit," I mutter, looking up to see that the light has changed to green. I step on the gas and rev through the intersection.

The phone and Kira's response (or lack thereof) will have to wait.

Once I get to Rietta's, it takes me forever to fish my phone out of the thin sliver of space. Damn my muscular forearms. In most circumstances, I love how my engineering work has left me with a toned physique I don't have to work too hard for. However, in times like these, muscles are a nuisance.

Finally, I grab it and check my phone. No response from Kira. What the hell?

I shake it off. I'll give her shit for it when I see her.

I head into Rietta's. It's an authentic taco place, not one of those trendy bullshit restaurants that's not even owned by people with Mexican heritage. The plates are plastic, the horchata is fresh, and tacos are three dollars apiece (fuck inflation), which means I can order a platter full and be set for the rest of the day.

When I walk in, I'm greeted by a young hostess with full apple cheeks and jet black hair in two plaits over her shoulders. "One for lunch?"

"I'm actually meeting some people. Two girls," I say and then curse myself. *They're not girls. They're women.* "One blonde, one brunette." This sounds like the beginning of a porno.

The hostess frowns. "I'm not sure we have anyone like that seated right now."

"Is it okay if I just go take a look?" I say, pointing through the doorway to the dining room.

She smiles and nods. "Please, be my guest."

"Thanks."

I walk into the dining room which is decorated for Christmas, Mexico style. Poinsettias in every corner, papel picado in red and green along the walls, not to mention the very conspicuous nativity scene lining the front of the stage they use for late night mariachi. I scan the room for any sign of Kira and Dana, but the hostess was right. There are no two women here on their–

I stop in my tracks when my eyes land on a blonde sitting near the window with a cup of horchata half drunk in front of her. It's Dana. And she's alone, at a table set for two.

Suddenly, it all comes together.

"Kira, you little imp," I mutter to myself and smile. My feelings for Dana are obvious to everyone but Dana herself.

And I'm glad for it. The Solace sisters make great wing women.

Dana's eyes land on me and she waves, that signature glowing smile spreading across her lips.

"Just you?" I say on approach, though I'm celebrating inside.

Dana rolls her eyes and dunks her straw into the horchata, stirring the cinnamon up that's collected on the bottom. "Kira had a work thing come up."

I bet she did.

"Orlie is working her like a dog. I can't stand it," Dana mutters. "Anyway, are you just going to stand there?"

I laugh, shrug off my light jacket, and drop into my chair. "No, I'm starving."

"Good, I've already ordered," Dana says and then smiles, clasping her hands under her chin. "Hope that's okay."

Any good friend would know your order at a restaurant you go to regularly. And yet, Dana ordering on my behalf gives me a feeling of electricity in my chest.

Don't get ahead of yourself, Drew. It's just lunch.

"Better than okay. Perfect."

Subtle is not *my middle name...*

3

DANA

"God, I couldn't eat another bite," I say and then grab an al pastor taco off the platter in front of us.

"There's always room for al pastor, though," Drew says with a laugh.

I take a bite despite my stomach being on the verge of explosion, the pineappley porky goodness melting on my tongue. "Mm, you got that right."

Drew laughs at me, eyes wrinkling at the corners. His scruff is more trimmed than usual. Still scruffy, though. I'd be lying if I said I didn't want to touch his cheek and feel his facial hair just once. "You're hilarious, D."

"Takes one to know one, D."

Stupid little nickname that makes my stomach flip every time. This man might be the death of me.

"What are you doing tonight?" I ask and immediately regret it when I see how Drew's mouth falls ajar. "No reason, only curious." I'm deeply frightened of the day Drew says he's going on a date. If he dates, he doesn't tell me. Never asked me for advice or what to say to a girl who sent a cryptic text. I can't imagine he doesn't at least try. He's a catch.

"Um...I was probably just going to start packing for Maldives," he says with a shrug.

Drew is my plus one for Gillian and Axel's wedding. Gillian said she'd give Drew his own invitation, but I told her not to bother giving us plus ones. It wasn't like either of us was going to fall into serious relationships between August and December.

Plus, at least this way, if Drew *had* miraculously met the love of his life, I wouldn't have to deal with him being all happy and lovey at my sister's wedding.

"Or do a little work. I want to get started on some more drawings on this engine."

I roll my eyes. "What is it with all the workaholics around here?"

Drew grins. "I'm sorry!"

"Everyone's always working or with their kids or on dates or–" I stop and shake my head.

"Did you want to do something tonight? I could–"

"No, no. You have to *work*."

"Dana, come on, don't be that way," Drew says and then crunches on a chip dipped in salsa verde.

I sigh. "I'm not...Sorry."

"We could go see a movie or hit up a show. I'm not married to my work."

The use of the word married right now makes the hairs on the back of my neck stand on end.

He narrows his eyes, dark blue obscured in shadow. "What's wrong?"

I raise my eyebrows. I shouldn't be surprised. Two years of friendship is nothing to shake a stick at. You can learn people really fast when you care to. "Nothing."

"You're lying."

I put down my half-eaten taco and wipe the juice off my fingers. "I remember when I would have said that to you."

"Guess I had a good teacher when it comes to reading people," he says with a half-smile.

Back when I was counseling him, I remember how surprised Drew would be when I was able to pinpoint something going on in his brain he hadn't said out loud. It's a blessing and a curse to know how people feel. On one hand, I feel like I can see the world very clearly. I'm able to read a room, make people feel safe, build and maintain close friendships because of how I'm able to care. And on the other hand, I'm always burdened with worry for others and don't think about myself enough.

Being in the business of emotions means I have to work hard at not being burnt out. My clients come to me with their heaviest emotional loads. I have to be on top of my game to receive them.

It's why counselors, therapists, and psychiatrists are all in therapy themselves. We need somewhere to be understood when we're doing so much understanding ourselves.

"What's up, D?"

I look down at the demolished platter of tacos, trails of salsa, onions, and cilantro sprinkled across it. "It just hit me today how all my sisters are..." I meet his gaze and try to smile. "Growing up."

Drew's lips twist to the side. "That must be hard."

"Not hard, necessarily. I'm happy for them. You know I am."

"Of course."

"They all deserve everything. The whole world. You know I think that."

Drew shakes his head. "You never have to defend yourself to me, Dana."

My muscles relax. At least I don't have to worry about being misunderstood when I'm with Drew. He knows me. Knows my heart. "I think I'm feeling kind of lonely," I say in a small voice. "Feels stupid, but–"

"You can be surrounded by people and still feel like no one sees you. I know how that feels," he says.

Drew's voice is so kind. I've always thought this. From the second he stepped into my office; I was surprised to feel like I was talking to another counselor. Makes his peptalks and advice sessions even more impactful.

"I feel like they don't need me anymore," I say, picking at the tablecloth.

"*Dana.*"

"Seriously. They don't. Harley has Grant, Gillian has Axel, Amy has Hunter. Who knows what happens next with Kira? The only one who might actually need me is my dad and he doesn't actually really need me because, well, he's my dad, and even if he *did* need me, he wouldn't say it. So, that leaves me, and–"

Drew's hand darts out and captures my own on the table. "Dana, you're talking a mile a minute. Take a breath."

I sit there and stare at our hands. Drew has touched me before. Given me a high five, a playful shove, a hug. Grabbing my hand across the table, though?

That's not a friend thing to do.

And the way his thumb is trailing across the back of my hand with tenderness...that's *definitely* not a friend thing to do.

"Your sisters will always need you. You're irreplaceable, Dana. I promise."

Does that mean that *Drew* thinks I'm irreplaceable too?

My heart is beating in my throat. If he doesn't let go soon enough, I might just lean across this table and kiss him. And that would ruin everything, wouldn't it?

I yank my hand away suddenly and smile nervously. "Yeah, you're right. Thanks. You're...Thank you."

Drew's brow tightens for only a moment before he retracts his hand and sticks it in his lap. "Yeah, of course. Any time."

An awkward silence falls over us as Spanish pop music plays in the background. I scoop up the rest of my al pastor taco and stuff it in my mouth. Drew chuckles as I chew and I try to smile with my mouth packed full.

I need to figure out what I want. Because if it's really Drew, I'm squandering every opportunity to have him.

I TURN OVER IN BED. I can smell him in the pillow, his musk mixed with cologne mixed with grease.

I feel a hot breath on the inside of my thigh and look down at the sheets. "What are you doing?"

He kisses the inside of my thigh. "Waking you up."

My mouth grows hot. "Drew, what are you–"

He hushes me and plants a hand to my lower belly. "Just relax. Let me take care of you."

Memory is not serving me right now. I don't know how I got here, into my bed, and I certainly don't know how Drew got here either.

But I'm not going to fight it. Especially not when I feel his breath now against my lower lips.

"Smell so good, baby."

My entire body bucks when he places a kiss to the apex of my pubic bone. He chuckles. "Taste so good too."

I look down at the covers. Drew is merely a lump beneath them, obscured entirely by my comforter. I try to lift it up to watch him, but he doesn't let me. "*Relax...*" he hisses again, a cobra threatening to strike.

Drew's tongue flicks into my wet center and I let out a pleased moan.

This feels...different. I've been eaten out before. However, the way Drew is lapping up my juices and ensnaring my clit with his tongue is creating a warm numbness across my entire body.

How did I get here? I still don't understand.

However, I follow his instructions, spreading my arms back over my head and falling into the deep well of my bed. My entire body melts underneath him. Since I can't see him, every sensation is new. The way he caresses my hips or nuzzles his nose against my pubic hair. The feeling of a hot breath sliding up my belly or a soft rumble from his lower belly.

It feels *so good*.

"Dana..." he says and then repeats my name a few more times before delving his face between my legs again and pushing my thighs back.

"Drew, oh my god." I'm starting to tremble. All of my muscles are enslaved to the pleasure he's creating between my legs.

He thrusts his tongue into me almost like he's fucking me.

I can't even remember when he kissed me.

"I'm going to–"

Drew growls into my wetness.

"It's h-happening," I stutter, about to tip over the edge. "Let me watch when I–"

I grab the covers again. This time he doesn't hold them

down. I whip them back, but instead of Drew's beautiful mouth clamped around my clitoris, all I see is blackness.

Nothing.

And in the blink of an eye, my orgasm is yanked away and the blackness swallows me whole.

My entire body jerks awake. I'm sweating all over. Light is streaming in through the blinds. *Fuck, what time is it?*

I grab my phone off the nightstand. It's already half past eight. Shit. I was supposed to be up a half hour ago. I'm meeting all my sisters at the bakery to discuss all the last minute details before we go to Maldives in two days and I wanted to get there early to chat with Gillian and see how she's feeling about everything and what I can do to help.

However, it looks like I'm just going to make it in the nick of time.

I leap out of bed and into the shower, washing the sweat off as well as the guilt. Dear god, where did that dream come from?

I'd be lying if I said I hadn't dreamed of Drew before. I mean, we spend so much time together, it's not *unusual*.

In the past, though, the most we've done is kiss...maybe touch. Not *that*.

Thank god my subconscious didn't give me the full image of what Drew would look like between my legs. That might have been too much to bear.

Guilt is not as easy to cleanse as sweat, so I'm still stewing in it by the time I get to Gillian's vegan bakery. All my sisters are there along with Lola, Gillian's best friend and maid of honor. Much easier to choose someone not in the family than to deal with all her sisters scrambling for the title of "best sister" (even if Harley snagged "matron of honor." Although, whether or not being a "matron" is an honor, none of us are sure yet).

"So, we're flying private out of LAX Monday morning. We have four private jets that–"

"Jeez, Gilly, you didn't tell me he had *that* kind of money," Amy whispers.

Lola blushes and looks away. Lola also happens to be Axel's sister which makes this even more of a family affair. The Hitchins family property dynasty is generations old. And generational wealth is no joke.

"Don't act like Hunter doesn't run resorts on every continent, Amy," Harley snorts.

"Are we playing ring around the rosy of billionaires or talking about Gillian's wedding?" Kira snaps.

"Thank you, Kiki," Gillian says with a smile. "Anyway, the wedding planner suggested that we mix everyone up in order to give a feeling of camaraderie to the wedding. After all, all the guests are going to be there for at least five days. It'll just be family and close friends, but we want everyone to feel welcome."

Amy screws her lips together. "Are you saying we're cliquey?"

"Amy, *shush*," I say and smack her thigh.

"We'll put you with your plus ones, obviously, but–"

"Don't worry about me," I intercede impulsively.

Everyone looks at me. A bunch of brown eyes (and Lola's blue ones) staring with confusion.

"You should separate Drew and me. To...you know, mix it up," I say.

"You don't want to fly with Drew?" Harley asks. "You're just going to throw him to the wolves?"

I laugh. "He's a big boy, he can make some new friends. Who knows, he might meet someone he–"

There is a collective groan. "Dana, enough of this pretending you want Drew to find a girlfriend! I'm sick of it," Amy says, spreading her hands wide in an "enough" motion.

I frown. "I do. Of course, I do."

"Just admit you like him," Amy says.

"I *do* like him. As a friend."

Another collective groan. My eyes dart from sister to sister to Lola, hoping someone will be on my side. Not even Kira, my quietest, most reserved sister is on my side. "Guys, seriously. We're not a thing." I look at Gillian and nod firmly. "I want Drew and I on different planes."

Gillian and Lola exchange a look before Gillian smiles in resignation. "Fine, Dana. Whatever you say."

Something tells me they're not going to make this trip easy for me when it comes to Drew.

4

———

DREW

I thought for sure I'd be on the same flight as Dana, but she had to be at the airport for takeoff half an hour before me. Not sure why Axel and Gillian are set on the flights being some sort of meet and greet, but that's how it's going to be.

I don't recognize anyone as I climb the stairs onto the jet.

When I hear the term private jet, I think of a tiny little thing where you're practically in the cockpit when you're in the bathroom. This, though, is practically the size of a commercial jet. It must have all sorts of amenities for about twenty-five people. After all, we're going to be in the air for nearly twenty-four hours.

Flying private has its perks, that's for sure. Beyond just the luxury of it, we can fly direct from LAX to Maldives which is impossible from any commercial airline in the US.

I shoulder my duffel and duck my head down to keep from brushing up against the lower clearance of the door.

"Welcome, Mr. Young," a young flight attendant with

bleached blonde hair says sweetly, handing me a glass of champagne.

I smile. "Have we met before?"

She smiles back, although it's not as humorous as mine. "No, but now we have. I'm Ingrid."

"Nice to meet you, Ingrid."

"Likewise."

I guess they must have studied our photos. All the crew seems to be addressing us by name. Must be a perk of being rich and well known. Although, I have to admit, it's a weird fucking perk.

"This is the lounge," she says, gesturing to the open barrel of the plane before me. "Beyond the red curtain—" she points to a curtain at the end of the lounge, "—are your lie-flat cabins. You've been assigned F-three. You can give your bag to Gerard here—"

Another attendant pops up, a man with curly hair that sticks straight out, almost like a clown. He holds out his hands for my bag with a undeterrable smile.

"—and he'll stow it in an overhead bin for you."

I swallow. Look, I've got money for nice things. Beyond just my work as an engineer, I've had some luck over the past few years with the market's volatility. I can afford first class and the works. However, I like to live frugally. I'm not better than anyone. Just ingrained in me from an early age.

"Don't worry!" Gerard grins. "Nothing is too heavy for me."

I half-smile and hand in the duffel. "Well, I'm a light packer."

Gerard takes it and scampers through the lounge, disappearing behind the red curtain.

"Please let us know if there is anything you need, Mr. Young," Ingrid says.

"Please, call me Drew. Don't need the formalities."

She smiles. "As you wish."

I give her one last nod, shuffle past her into the lounge, sipping on the champagne. Bet this stuff is expensive. Although I don't usually have a taste for champagne, so I wouldn't even know.

The "lounge" doesn't even look like the inside of a plane. Lush couches, a bar, oak tables jutting out of the wall. I can't wait to see what kind of lunch we'll be served once we take off. I'm starving.

I scan once more for any faces I recognize. I immediately lock eyes with Kira Solace and feel a smile spread across my face. Thank god. Someone I know. I raise my hand to greet her but am stopped by a harsh tug on my arm. I gasp and turn to look at the owner of the hand, ready to curse.

But I lose all ability to speak when I see her face.

"How long has it *been*, Drew?"

Willow Harcourt. My ex-girlfriend. She looks the same. Which is to say good. Nothing special. Her dark hair sits in a styled ponytail and her lashes are lathered in mascara. Looks much more suited to a runway than a near day-long plane ride. "Willow...what are you doing here?"

She giggles loudly as if she's trying to attract attention. It works, unfortunately. "I'm in the wedding party, of course!"

Of course...?

"Gillian and I went to grade school together. You remember that, don't you?" Willow asks. Her hand hasn't left my arm. "I got her sister's contact for you? The grief counselor?"

"Shit, that's right," I say, hoping I haven't turned paper-white as I stare at her.

"Did you ever go to her?"

I had kept Dana's name for a while before I reached out. In fact, I think I'd pushed it out of my memory that Willow was the one who'd given it to me. But one day, when grief over losing my mom got to be too much and I went to the fridge to grab a beer to numb the pain, I saw the business card again.

Dana Solace, Grief Counselor
Heal From Within

I drank the beer and then called. The rest is history now, clearly.

"Yeah, I did."

"Good. *Good.* You look good. You look happy. Are you on Zoloft?"

I chuckle.

"Prozac?" she guesses again.

"Wellbutrin," I reply.

She claps her hands. "That's a good one!"

The depression and the grief went hand in hand. Turned out I'd been dealing with the feeling of dread and lack of self-worth for a while before my mom passed. I'm on a low dose that keeps me even keeled. "I'm surprised Gillian didn't tell you that...that Dana was the one who invited me."

Willow snorts. "Well, Gillian and I are old friends, but that doesn't mean we catch up as often as we should. You know? Don't you have people you know that you might not see them for several years, but then you get into the same room and it's like..." She trails off. Her green eyes meet mine, trying to tell me something without words. It gives me the shivers. "...no time has passed?"

I shake my head. "Don't really have anyone like that, actually."

Her face falls ever so slightly, but then she forces a smile again. "Come on, let's sit. Catch up."

She practically tackles me onto a velvet couch. I manage not to spill the champagne. Thank god, because I'm going to need it to get through this conversation. I knock it back and then let Willow chat my ear off.

As I listen, or half listen, I see Kira across the room. My eyes plead for help, but she merely witnesses, apathetic. She must think I *want* to be sitting here, captive by Willow. Quite the contrary. There's a reason we broke up, after all.

And to be honest, the reasons aren't that deep. My mom died. The relationship was already on the rocks. I pulled away and then cut her off completely. I think I knew from the beginning it wouldn't be forever. Willow wanted things I didn't. A traditional type of guy with a traditional career, someone who would move out to Orange County and support her career as a housewife and future mother.

Don't get me wrong, those are formidable things to want. People should be whatever they want to be. However, I was twenty-eight. I couldn't even fathom a mortgage, let alone a wife and child. Child*ren* if Willow had anything to say about it.

It just made sense to let her go along with my mother. Start completely fresh.

"So, when I heard Gillian was getting married, I just had to be in the party. You know?"

Just like Willow to *ask* to be in a wedding party. "Of course."

"I mean, Gillian, Lola, and I were like...the Power Puff Girls or something."

"Which one were you?" I ask.

Willow giggles and leans into my ear. "Guess."

I'm not drunk enough for this.

"Everyone, we will be getting ready to taxi. Please make your way to your seats. Once we are in the air, we will begin lunch service," Ingrid announces.

Perfect timing.

To my chagrin, Willow has somehow weaseled her seat next to mine. I was actually supposed to be beside Kira, but Willow came up and begged and begged. "We're catching up. Old times, you know?"

Kira looked to me for permission. But what was I going to do? Shake my head? Give her a thumbs down? I merely shrugged. Thought she might get the message.

She didn't.

Luckily, the seats are wide, another perk of the private plane lifestyle. That doesn't stop Willow from leaning onto the arm of my seat the whole time we're taxiing and all the way through takeoff.

"Oooh! I love that moment where the wheels leave the ground!" she announces to me, her voice much too loud for the nearly silent plane.

"Yeah, me too," I say and lean my head back. Maybe if I close my eyes, she'll get the idea that I don't want to talk.

"God, do you remember the last time we took a trip together?"

Guess not. "Oh yeah. It was–"

"It was Costa Rica. Remember that?"

I sigh. That was the beginning of the end in my memory. Her taste at the time was much too much for where I was financially. I have to do my best not to show my hand that now, I'm several tax brackets ahead of where I used to be. "I do."

"Oh, it was such a nice trip." I feel her breath on my ear. "A *very* nice trip."

I pop my eyes open. Willow is an inch away from me, grinning. I jerk away and laugh nervously, pressing myself up against the window. Why couldn't I have had the aisle seat? Then I could have escaped. "Y-yeah."

"Although, we didn't see as much of the island as I would have liked. So much time in the hotel..." Willow practically purrs.

I clear my throat.

"So, tell me, Drew, honey. Have you missed me?"

I stare at her. The answer is no. In fact, it's hell no. However, I know how she can get when her feelings are hurt. Vicious. And I don't want to ruin this for Axel and Gillian. Even if they're not on the plane, I don't want to expose their guests to her madness. She could create a one-woman massacre to rival the one in Boston in the eighteenth century. I have to think fast. Have to say something to get her off my case. "Yeah, Willow, about that...I should tell you something. Something important."

5

DANA

Ricks Maldives is...incredible. It looks more like a movie set than the ones I've seen on Grant's soundstages.

The entire resort is situated on an atoll, a series of bungalows attached by long, swirling docks. Of course, I only saw all of that from the boat ride over. I can't wait to get all up close and personal with my own private bungalow.

The entrance to the resort is sheathed in tropical trees and foliage, giving us respite from the bright sun. The weather in Maldives this time of year is perfect. The beginning of dry season, very little rain, bright sun, but not melting hot.

Gillian and I walk in, holding Stella's hands, one on each side. "This is...incredible," I mutter.

"I know. What a better way to get married, right?"

I could think of plenty better ways. In the backyard of our childhood home for instance. However, this is perfect for Gillian. So much nature all around, sea breezes, and beautiful views.

"Can we go to the pool?" Stella asks, jumping up and down between us.

"How do you have so much energy, goodness gracious," I murmur. Sure, we were able to sleep on the plane, but plane-sleeping is much different than actual bed-sleeping.

"One thing at a time, sweetheart. We have to check in first."

Suddenly, Stella lets go of our hands and cries out, "Daddy!" She bolts toward the front desk where Axel stands waiting for us in a nice linen suit. He already looks like he's gotten a tan even though he hasn't been here more than an hour.

With Stella no longer between us, Gillian grabs my hand as we walk. "Thanks for being my rock through this, Dana," she whispers.

I shake my head. "Don't be silly."

"You are. You really are."

I smile at Gillian. Most of the flight, she was trying not to panic. Suddenly, her whirlwind romance with Axel was moving too fast for her. "What if I'm making a mistake?" she squeaked while we were both locked in the bathroom, which was quite a feat of contortion.

Cold feet, I've learned, is natural. Harley suffered the same thing before marrying Grant. I expected Gillian to be twice as bad. After all, she's not just making a decision for her, but for Stella too.

However, judging by how Axel has Stella all coiled up in his arms, hugging her tightly, it would be shocking to think this was anything *but* a good decision.

"And there's my beautiful wife-to-be," Axel announces as we approach him.

"Don't be mushy, Axel." Gillian lets go of my hand and

throws her arms around her little family. I feel a pang in my chest. I shouldn't be feeling this. The pang of her walking into the next phase of her life should be saved exclusively for Dad. However, I can't help it. She's moving on. I'm so happy for her.

And yet...that emptiness.

"Hi, Dana," Axel says and gives me a kiss on the cheek.

"How was your flight?" I ask.

He sighs with a smile. "Great. Even better now that I can stretch my legs." He bobs up and down, Stella laughs. "I've already checked us in. How about I take Stella ahead and you can–"

"You all go. Enjoy it," I say.

Gillian looks at me carefully. "You sure?"

"Of course. It's just a hotel check-in. I'll be fine."

My sister smiles with the brightness of a child about to go to Disneyland. "Okay, let's go."

And just like that, I've been replaced with Axel on Stella's other side. They walk hand in hand. The three of them.

As it should be.

"Brunch at eleven at the lagoon!" Axel shouts over his shoulder. "Don't forget!"

"You're a member of the Hitchins and Solace party, ma'am?"

I turn to the man behind the front desk.

Ma'am? I'm only thirty. Do I look like a ma'am? "Yes, I am."

The man smiles. "Let me get you checked in, then. Could I have your name?"

I lean my arms on the desk. "Dana Solace."

He types some and then grins. "Dana Solace and Drew Young. Yes, I have you right here."

I frown. "Wait, I–"

"Is he with you now?" he asks.

I blink. "Um, no, he's–"

"Would you like me to save a key here for him or just send him to meet you at your bungalow."

I shake my head.

Wait a second. Rewind. "I'm sorry, the room should just be for Dana Solace."

The desk manager clutches his heart. "Is he no longer attending?"

"No, no. It's just we–we should have separate bungalows."

"Separate?"

I nod. "Yes, separate."

"You did not come together?"

"We are–he's–we're coming together, but–" *Dana, seriously? Coming?* "I mean, he's my plus one, but we aren't *together.*"

The desk manager pouts his lips. *Shit, he doesn't get it.*

"What I mean is...Drew Young is my guest. But he's not my romantic guest. He's a friend. Coming as my date. You know?"

Realization bursts across the man's face. "Oh! You're not lovers, then?"

Lovers?! This has got to be some sort of Candid Camera Punk'd bullshit! "No, we're not."

"Well, I'm afraid I have you down as lovers."

"Is that what it says on your computer?" I gape.

"Forgive me, you are on the same reservation. That's all."

I take a deep breath. I wonder who is responsible for this. Is this one of my sister's sick version of a joke? Hunter trying to play matchmaker? Or is this a genuine fuckup that just couldn't be helped? I look in the direction Gillian, Axel, and Stella left. They're a mere memory at this point, the archway toward the dock taunting me. Best not to bother them.

I can stomach this, even if it's weird. Even if it shouldn't be happening. This isn't my wedding. I'm not going to make a problem of something that's not. Because Drew and I staying in a room together...that's not a problem. Right?

"Yes, of course, that's fine," I say, waving my hands in front of my face.

"Oh, good," he says with a heavy sigh. "I was nervous that your visit was already dissatisfactory."

I smile. "No, not a chance. Thank you for your attentiveness, though."

The man hands me a keycard and explains my bags have already been taken to the room. Then, he hands me a laminated itinerary. "This is the itinerary for the wedding week. I hope you have a pleasant stay. If you need anything, please don't hesitate to ask."

I thank him and start to walk away. But I'd be remiss not to ask. "Just in case, you don't have any other bungalows available do you?"

The man pouts out his lower lip. "I'm afraid not."

Of course not. I shrug. "Had to ask." Then I walk (no, *run*) through the archway and down the dock to bungalow twenty-eight. The thing sure looks big enough for two people. We can probably make this work.

I scan the card, open the door, and feel my stomach drop when I see the big bed in the middle of the room, draped with a mosquito net across from a set of glass doors that open onto a personal-sized pool and then the wide expanse of the Indian Ocean.

The view and amenities don't matter, though, because I'm concerned with one and only thing.

There is one bed. And unless I'm an asshole and make Drew sleep on the couch that is clearly not long enough to fit him, we're going to have to share it.

This is going to be a long couple of weeks.

6

———

DREW

My plane group tears into the resort with sweat on our brows. The boat that was supposed to take us from the airport island to the resort was late, and on top of that, didn't have air conditioning inside. I need a shower immediately. However, according to Kira, we're already late for the first festivities and Gillian is freaking out. Must attend the bride first and foremost, especially as a date to someone in the wedding party.

Admittedly, when Dana first asked me to attend the wedding, I couldn't help but think it was something of a romantic thing. I mean, who takes a friend as a plus one to a wedding? Dana Solace, that's who.

Of course, she's my best friend. I'd never say no.

We're shuffled quickly down to the beach, our bags shoveled away from us and to our rooms. God, I'd love to just collapse on my bed and take a breath. Enjoy a moment away from *Willow* because she's been talking my ear off nearly the whole twenty hours we were in the air because she has a hard time sleeping on planes.

However, once we walk onto the beach to the lagoon

side restaurant, I breathe a sigh of relief. For one, the view is spectacular. I've never seen water so blue or skies so wide.

More importantly, though, I see Dana sitting near the head of the main table with her sisters, their partners, and the wedding party.

I didn't realize how badly I needed to see her after this odyssey to get here.

As if sensing me, she sees me almost immediately. There's a panicked look on her face. Something's wrong. Although, I'm not sure what.

Thankfully, Willow doesn't make a fool of me by grabbing onto my arm, rather she floats gracefully to the table and kisses Gillian on the cheek eagerly and then Stella. Stella is less than pleased.

As I approach the table, Dana stands and comes toward me.

Why is my heart throbbing? She's coming so quickly I nearly expect her to run up to me and kiss me, which would be *more* than welcome. It'd be–

"We have a problem," she says through gritted teeth, grabbing my hand and yanking me back to the boardwalk.

"Whoa, whoa, whoa, slow down!" I cry out.

But Dana is a woman on a mission and doesn't stop until we are well out of earshot of any human soul, shaded by some palm trees.

"Hello to you too," I say in a monotone voice.

Dana flushes. "Sorry. Hello. How was your trip?"

I half-smile. "I'll tell you all about it when you don't have that look on your face."

Her eyebrows jump. "What look?"

"You know. Your worried look. Like–" I furrow my brow and puff up my cheeks.

That gets her to smile. "I don't look like I've got a balloon in my mouth."

"Sure do!"

"Drew!" Dana reaches out and slaps my arm.

"Okay, okay! What? What's wrong? We're in paradise, what could be wrong?"

Dana takes a deep breath and sighs. "They booked us in the same room."

I stare at her for a moment before bursting with laughter.

"*Drew.*"

"I'm sorry, that's funny. You have to admit that's funny."

Dana shakes her head. "It's not funny, it's—"

"It'll be like a slumber party," I say.

"We're too old for slumber parties."

"No, we're not. Come on. Where's your sense of adventure, D?"

She huffs. "Drew, this is not an adventure, this is a mistake. A big one. We should have been booked in different rooms. We have different last names, for crying out loud. It's not—"

"People who are together don't always share the same last name, Dana," I scoff.

Dana stares back at me.

"I mean. Not that we're—you know what I mean. Amy and Hunter for instance."

She sighs, crossing her arms over her chest, and looks away.

I don't like how worked up she is about this. Is it really so bad to share a room with me?

"There's only one bed, Drew."

Don't get hard...don't get hard... "We can put a barrier of pillows between us." She doesn't seem enthused by that. "Or I'll sleep on the floor."

Dana finally cracks a smile. "You will not sleep on the floor."

I look over my shoulder. This might work out in my favor more than Dana even knows at this point. "It'll be okay. I'll get on a list for a new room. And if there aren't any, I'm sure there will be some once the guests leave and it's just the rest of us for New Year's. Okay?"

"It's just so silly. I don't even know how this happened."

"I promise, I don't have cooties or anything. And I don't snore."

She glares.

"What?"

"That's not true."

My eyebrows jump. "I don't!"

"You do. I've watched enough movies with you to know *that* much."

I start to protest, but then shake my head. "You really think you know me that well, huh?"

Her arms over her chest go from defensive to proud. "I know you better than you think, D."

"Well, do you know me well enough to know I'll do *THIS?!*" I lunge toward her and start to tickle her sides.

Dana lets out a loud, screaming laugh. "Drew! Stop, I'm ticklish, I'm ticklish. Sto–hahahaha!" She bats me away, a big smile now on her face.

"So, did you expect that?" I ask.

Dana tilts her head to the side. And I suddenly realize how close I've gotten to her in our little private palm alcove. She shakes her head. "Fine. You got me. This time."

Her lips are close enough to kiss. Should I just get it over with? Just give us both permission to...No. If I kiss her and she hates it, we have two whole weeks to spend in a hotel room together. In the same fucking bed. I can't make things weird. Not now.

But damn, her glossy lips are enticing.

"We...should go back," she says, gingerly touching my chest to move past me.

I resist grabbing her hand and holding it there.

Dana Solace, you'll be the death of me.

We walk back down the boardwalk to the lagoon side restaurant. There is a din of chatter, silverware clinking, and the tide swishing up on the beach. Kira and Willow have made themselves comfortable at the family table, leaving two open spots for Dana and me. Not together, sadly.

When I get to the table, I'm greeted with warm welcomes from the Solaces and the wedding party. Everyone except Willow. I feel her glare on me as I sit down.

"What was that about?" she asks.

I give her a look. "Why do you think it's any of your business?"

She narrows her eyes and then grabs her mimosa.

The entire meal, I find my eyes drifting back to Dana. And every time I see her beautiful face, I imagine waking up next to it. I want to see her hair mussed from a night in bed, want to smell her morning smell, want to know how warm she feels when–

"So, Drew, Dana said you're working on a new project!" Kent cries out, clearly a few mimosas deep. "Tell us about it."

There's nothing better to kill an erotic fantasy than the dad of the girl you're thinking about asking you about work.

"I'm glad you asked, Kent."

7

______

DANA

I FEEL LIKE A PIECE OF FRIED CHICKEN BY THE TIME I get back to the bungalow. Brunch by the lagoon turned into an afternoon pool party at the main pool which basically meant just more day drinking under cabanas in our bathing suits.

I spent most of the time in the pool with the kids to give the moms a break. Between keeping Tana balanced in her floatie and being demanded to watch Stella do handstand after handstand, I'm fucking beat.

Thank goodness we have a few hours before we have to go to dinner. I need to digest all the delicious food and rest my eyes.

This trip is going to take way more out of me than I originally thought.

I toss my towel onto the entryway floor, followed by my bikini. Then, I head straight to the shower. The steam rehydrates my chlorine sapped skin. Feels so good after all the traveling. I feel the tiredness in every part of my body. It aches.

I take a few deep breaths. I'll feel better after a nap. And if I don't, I'll feel better in the morning.

After a long shower, I towel off and drop that on the floor too. It's a hotel. I can afford to be a little messy now and then.

"Shit," I say to myself when I realize I left the hotel provided robe out in the main room earlier. Oh well. I strut into the main room, running my hands through my hair and yawning.

"Oh, my god, Dana!"

I scream and duck down behind the bed before I can even fully process what's happening.

Drew is in the room.

How did I forget after all that fucking consternation that *Drew* is sharing a room with me? "Did you see anything?"

"N-not a lot."

I peek up over the bed. He's standing in front of the open door, still in his trunks, a towel around his neck and his Hawaiian shirt hanging open, revealing his chest. God, what a beautiful chest. Dark swirls of hair, taut pecs and abs, a scar from when he had his appendix removed as a child that I'd love to feel against my lips just once.

Dear god, what is happening to me?

"You're lying," I say.

"Well, you walked in here as if you owned the place, how was I supposed to know you'd be..." He gestures errantly toward me and then sighs. "Sorry, I'll knock next time or–"

I rest my forehead against the bed. "Could you close the door?"

"Sorry, sorry, I'm so–" I hear the door latch heavily.

"This is so embarrassing."

"Trust me, you're not as embarrassed as I am."

Was it really so embarrassing for him to see me naked? Am I hideous? "Can you hand me my robe?" I ask, holding my hand up over the bed, keeping myself concealed from plain view.

I hear him shuffling around for a minute before he finally comes upon the robe and tosses it my way. It lands right in my hand. "Good throw," I mumble and throw it over my shoulders like a cloak.

"Thanks. I watch baseball."

I can't hold back a snort of laughter. "Shut up." I tie the robe around my waist and pop up from behind the bed. Drew's eyes are downcast on the ground. "I'm not naked anymore. You can look."

"I know you're not, I just..." His jaw tenses. His Adam's apple bobs.

"What?"

Drew shakes his head. "Nothing. I'm going to take a shower." Except he doesn't move. Not even one inch.

"Why are you being weird?"

"I'm not being weird."

"Yeah, you are. Why won't you look at me?"

Drew lifts his eyes toward me but doesn't stop until he's looking at the ceiling.

"Still not looking at me."

"Yeah, I know, I just...I can't. Sorry."

His weirdness is suddenly quite charming. I'm making him nervous. I'm standing in the way of the bathroom and he's just seen me naked. Now I'm some sort of mythical creature he's afraid to make eye contact with. Medusa but without the turning to stone part. "Drew..."

"Dana..."

"Stop being weird and talk to me."

"I don't want to say it."

"Why?"

"Because–"

"Because..."

He tightens his hands on the ends of the towel around his neck. "I don't want to make things weird."

"They're already weird. Just say it."

Drew's eyes fall again and this time they settle right in mine. He looks like he's in pain. "If I look at you, I'm going to think about y-your breasts."

My face flushes. "You saw my breasts?"

He nods in shame.

I smile crookedly. How can a full-grown man that looks like *that* get so flustered when he sees a woman's breasts. "What did you think?"

His eyes widen.

"I mean–" *Oh god. Backtrack. That was weird.* I couldn't help it, though. He's here and I'm here and he saw my breasts and now I know he's thinking about them. "Sorry, that was–"

"Nice, they were nice. I mean, they were..." Drew gulps. "Really nice."

I purse my lips, trying not to smile like an idiot. Guys have seen me naked before. They've enjoyed my breasts before. So, why is it making me feel stupid in the head that Drew likes them? "You thought my tits were really nice?"

"I didn't say tits."

"That's not the part I care about, Drew."

I have made this situation sufficiently cryptic enough that I could back out now if I wanted to. But I don't want to. I'm usually not so impulsive. I am the type of person to measure every situation from all directions. Fuck that, though.

He's here and I'm here. We're in a room we have to share for two weeks. In one of the most gorgeous locations in the world.

I start to undo the closure on my robe and walk toward him.

"What are you doing," he whispers. Not a question, but almost a statement. He knows what I'm doing.

"If you can't tell me, I want you to show me. What you think of my tits," I murmur and then undo the tie on my robe so it comes apart, revealing my naked body to him.

Any shyness disappears almost immediately when I see how his pupils dilate at the sight of me. "Dana, I...oh god."

I let the robe slide down to the ground.

"Just tell me what you want," he says, voice straining. "I can't do anything until you tell me *exactly* what you want because I don't want to misread the situation or make you uncomfortable or–"

"Drew, I'm literally standing in front of you naked."

I never imagined he would be so frightened. So concerned. It's endearing he cares so much about doing right by me. Makes me want him even more.

Fine. I'll make his job easy for him.

I wrap my arms around his neck and rise up onto my tiptoes. My chest touches his, skin to skin. This isn't how I pictured our first kiss. Because yes, I've pictured it even if I shouldn't. I thought it'd be something more urbane or common. A kiss as he drops me off at my house, or one while taking a walk after a romantic dinner.

Not naked in a hotel room we're accidentally sharing in Maldives.

But fuck what I've been imagining. Reality is much better than those silly dreams.

Though there is passion brewing inside me, the first

time I kiss him is quiet and chaste. His lips are delicate in return, not asking for too much, but not passive either. Drew kisses me back. His hands slide around my bare lower back, pulling me into him. His scruff brushes up against my cheeks.

And that one kiss turns into two and into three. Each one gets more aggressive each time our lips meet. By the fourth, Drew is holding me so tight in his arms I'm nearly off the ground, and his tongue has slipped between my lips, devouring me with his kiss.

Now I can *really* imagine how his mouth would feel on each and every part of my body.

"Dana–" he whispers breathlessly.

I kiss him again, scraping my fingernails through his brown hair. "What?"

"I really want to–"

"Me too."

"Thank god."

In a fluid motion, Drew sweeps me off the ground and throws me onto the bed so I'm splayed out for him to see. He kneels on the edge, shaking off his shirt, tossing off the towel. All that's left are his shorts and removing those is *my job*.

I grab his waistband with my hand and tug them down. His cock springs out, completely hard. And it's big. Not intimidating. Just *perfect*. "Am I moving too fast?" I ask, meeting his gaze with mine but continuing to pull his shorts down his thighs.

"Faster than I thought you'd be, but–"

"You've thought about me?" I ask with a cocked smile.

"Is that not obvious at this point?"

I smile up at him and press a kiss to the bottom of his ribs. Drew tucks his hand through my hair as I trail kisses down to his navel. He melts into my control and, without much force, he sinks down onto the bed, falling onto his back so I'm on top of him.

My lips fall upon his appendix scar and I sigh happily.

"What?" he asks softly.

I trace my lips back and forth. It shouldn't be this easy to fall into intimacy with him. But it is. I know him so well. It was just a matter of time before his body became something I knew too. "You're beautiful, Drew."

"Not compared to you."

I lift my eyes and meet his over the plane of his body. He looks even more beautiful than before.

"Not compared to you, Dana," he repeats, shaking his head back and forth. "You're the *most* beautiful. The absolute—"

I take him off-guard, sliding my tongue along the ridge of his cock. Drew bucks, a dire gasp from between his lips. "Fuck...come on, Dana, why..."

I pop the head of his cock into my mouth and moan as I take him deeper. I've heard women often wonder what pleasure there is to be had out of giving a guy a blowjob. However, I know the trick. It also has to do with the man you're giving it to. And given how my feelings for Drew have been compounding on each other for two years now, not to mention just the past few days, it is an ultimate pleasure to please him.

As I run my lips up and down his shaft, Drew makes noises I could never have *dreamed* of. His tiny sighs of arousal, whimpers of delight, slight muttering of curses, and my name are all delicious.

I can taste him on the back of my tongue, precum leaking from the head.

Suddenly, he recoils his hips from me as best he can. I

take the hint, removing him from my mouth even though I wouldn't mind doing this for hours if he'd let me. I lift my gaze to him. Drew's usually self-assured expression is broken by a nervous smile and wide eyes.

"What?" I ask with a small giggle.

"You know what," he replies.

"You had me stop."

"Yes."

"Why?"

"Because I don't want to come in your mouth, Dana..." Drew says between heaving breaths.

A thrall of excitement flicks through my chest. He doesn't want to come in my mouth. He wants to come somewhere else.

"I didn't bring any condoms," he says sheepishly.

"That seems like poor planning for a single guy at a wedding."

Drew gets up on his elbows, ducking his head down. "I knew there wouldn't be anyone here I'd be interested in other than..."

Other than who? Say it. Please say it.

"And you know I'd never assume that...you and me."

I start to crawl up the length of his body so slowly and steady that the room is silent. I can't hear the ocean swishing outside or the sea breeze wafting through the curtains. All I can hear is our breath melting together. I straddle him, my face lingering over his. His eyes are glued to my lips. Such a polite guy, waiting for me to make every move.

It's his turn now. Just got to get him there.

"I didn't bring any condoms either," I whisper. "Because you're the only person here I knew I'd want to have sex with." I settle softly onto his pelvis, his hardness pressed into the notch of my groin. "I'm on the pill, though."

I hear him swallow. "So, what's that mean for me?"

I kiss his chin and drag my lips up to his mouth. "That you can be inside me. Bare."

"Oh god, Dana..." he groans.

"You can come inside me too. If you want." My confidence falters only momentarily. I don't want him to think I'm trying to make this something bigger than it is. For all I know, one round of sex will be enough to get it out of our system (although I pray that's not all it takes).

We linger for a moment, I'm about to find something else to say to fill the silence. However, Drew takes the lead. *Thank god.* He wraps his hand around the back of my head, smashing his lips to mine in a deep kiss. Our tongues tangle and tease, his teeth nibble on my lower lip. And just as I start to grind my hips against his, Drew takes ultimate control.

He flips me over onto my back, bracing his hands on either side of my head. Our eyes meet, a primal look of need. His biceps bulge. "You ready?" he asks.

All I can do is nod. Because I'm ready, but I'm also not. This seems like the final threshold before our friendship is entirely not a friendship anymore.

"Guide me," he says.

I pull my knees back to give him a wider entrance, then slide the head of his cock back and forth through my slick center. It's a sort of awkward dance, but Drew makes it easy with his lopsided smile. "Almost," I say. Then, his head hits my entrance perfectly. I shift my hips back. "There, you can..."

Before Drew pushes into me, he touches my jaw tenderly, his thumb resting on my chin, right below my lip. "We can stop whenever you want. If it's too much or…"

"I know," I nod and kiss his thumb.

"Yeah? Good. I won't be upset or—"

"Drew, I want you inside me. Please." My voice is barely audible at this point. All the energy in my body is directed to my blushing lower lips. They are eager, wanting, throbbing for him to be inside me. I'd beg if he made me.

Drew takes a deep breath; his eyes don't leave mine as he slides inside until it becomes too much to bear and he closes them tight.

The stretch stings at first, but with each passing moment, I relax, welcoming him inside. And once Drew has made that first stroke, my body knows this is exactly right.

Like we were made for each other.

"This okay?" he asks, attempting to keep his voice even, slowly pumping his hips.

I tuck my hands under his ass, tight and full. Why is he always hiding it in those baggy jeans? "You can go faster."

He does.

I ride the tide of his thrusts, over and over, my body bobbing through the sheets. Feels so good the deeper he goes. I couldn't have imagined how wonderful he'd feel, especially whenever our eyes meet. Because despite the primal nature of the act, his eyes are full of admiration and gentleness.

I tuck my hand around his neck, twirling my fingers through the slight tail his hair makes at the base of his skull. "Feel so good, baby."

He hums. "I like when you call me baby."

"Yeah?"

Drew leans down so his face hovers over mine. "I'm going to make you feel so good."

Before I can respond, his hips jerk faster, his cock sliding in and out of me. A knot forms at the base of my throat and my eyes widen. I try to moan, but I can't. It's locked inside me, pleasure robbing me of my sentence.

I lock my hands around his shoulders, pulling his chest up against mine, and twist my ankles around his tailbone. We trade the same breath back and forth, lips longing to kiss, but in need of space as we build together to something...something extraordinary.

"Fuck, you're amazing," he curses through clenched teeth.

"Look at me."

Eyes lock. Heartbeats match, bumping wildly. My fingernails dig into his skin. I wish he could be closer even though he's as close as possible to me.

Drew's mouth forms into a tight line and his brow furrows. Thrust after thrust after thrust, I feel myself building closer and closer and closer until–

"Dana, you're going to make me–"

"You're going to make *me*!"

And just as he lets out a raw laugh, my body snaps, orgasm bursting without warning. I push my mouth up against his collarbone and moan, no, scream with ecstasy. Tears come to my eyes. I can't help it. It feels so good.

"Shit, are you–oh god, you–" Drew can't get a straight question out before he comes, unable to withstand the clenching of my pussy around him. His head drops into the bed beside me, a long moan mismatched with the pulses of his cock inside me.

I cling to him, holding him to my chest, my contorted lips against his chest turning into light kisses.

Drew lets out one more strangled moan and then lifts his mouth to my ear. "You okay?"

"Okay would be an understatement."

I can hear the smile on his lips. "Did you enjoy it?"

I turn my head toward him. "Yes, baby."

His eyes roll upward, a flushed grin on his face. "I can't get enough of that." Then, he sighs. "Can't get enough of you."

"Well, good," I say and then kiss his nose. "Because you can have as much of me as you like."

8

DREW

Dana fell asleep on my chest. Her lips are right up against my nipple, hanging open as she snores lightly. It's darling.

I haven't been able to join her in sleep. I'm still in shock over everything that's gone down between us in the past two hours.

I always knew I'd enjoy sex with Dana. But I didn't know she had a vixen buried inside her, under that saintly exterior. More than that, though, I got to be close to her in a way I've dreamed about for much longer than I care to admit.

She's my dream girl. Plain and simple.

I push my lips against the crown of her head, blonde curls tickling my nose. I take a deep breath; the eucalyptus shampoo mixed with sweat is like an aphrodisiac. However, I'm not going to wake her up just for my little whim of arousal. This moment, right here, is heaven.

Underneath the euphoria that we have finally found our way into each other's arms, however, is terror.

I don't want to fuck this up.

But...I'm pretty sure I already have.

See, twenty plus hours on a plane is, shocker, a lot of fucking time.

With Willow in my ear for most of it, it felt like a lifetime. And given how obvious she made it that she had her sights set on me, after all these years of being broken up, I had to find some way to make her back off.

"So, what's Drew been up to? What makes Drew tick these days?" she had asked, leaning on the space between our seats, so close I could smell her sickly sweet perfume.

I chewed on my lower lip. "Working."

"Just work? No play?"

Right at that moment, Kira had walked by and shot daggers at me with her eyes. *You better not pull anything that would hurt my sister.* Dana's sisters have always, *always* understood my feelings for Dana. In fact, I outright told Gillian once. I'm sure there's a sisterly code of conduct that prevents secrets from being well and truly kept.

Regardless, they're rooting for me. Rooting for *us.* And so am I.

So, I wasn't going to let Willow jeopardize the possibility of Dana and me being a thing in the future.

"Some play. I'm actually seeing someone," I told Willow.

Her eyebrows leaped upward. "What?" Her shock and disappointment were obvious.

I forced a smile. "Yeah, you remember Gillian's sister?"

"You're dating your *grief counselor?!*"

"She's not my grief counselor anymore. We had to stop things when I...caught feelings." This isn't entirely untrue. I did stop things when I started having feelings for her. We just didn't stop so we could date. "We've been together for a while. Otherwise, why would I be invited to this wedding?" I went on with a soft laugh.

Needless to say, this made Willow back off. At least a little. She still attempted a flirtation here and there and teased me from time to time about my "relationship" with Dana, disdain filling her voice.

But it helped. It made that flight *bearable*.

However, when she mentioned it to Kira during dinner, Kira demanded an explanation.

"You're pretending to be in a relationship with my sister to get your ex-girlfriend to leave you alone?" she whispered to me in the middle of the night while everyone else was asleep. She'd told me to meet her by her seat at midnight and no one says no to Kira Solace (or any of her sisters for that matter).

I sighed, "I had to."

"How about get into an *actual* relationship with my sister. And then you can claim that title," Kira said.

I gulped. "Pretending is so much easier, though."

Kira rolled her eyes. "When this all falls apart, I'm not covering for you."

"Fair enough."

So now, here I am, in bed with the girl I lied about being in a relationship with even though I'd actually love to be in a *real* relationship with her, and the only people who know about this fake long-term relationship are her sister and my ex-girlfriend. All at a wedding.

I'm not a fan of complications, but I'm miraculously good at them.

As if sensing my exponentially stressful thoughts, Dana shifts in my arms. Her naked breasts brush up against me. "Mm."

I rub her back softly. "Welcome back, sleepyhead."

She lifts her head and screws her eyes together, adjusting to the light. A smile appears on her face. "Hi."

"Hi."

Dana kisses me softly.

"Mm..." Her lips feel so good against mine.

"What time is it?" she asks, her head drooping again onto my shoulder.

I look over on my nightstand and grab the hotel alarm clock. "Shit. Twenty to eight."

Dana shoots up from her spot on my chest in shock. "What?! How did you let me sleep so long?" She jumps out of bed, her naked body looking fantastic tinged in Maldivian sunset.

"You were so cozy; how could I wake you up?" I say with a grin.

Dana sorts through her suitcase, throwing things on the floor. Floral dresses, brightly colored sarongs, a few thongs I wouldn't mind taking *off* of her if circumstances allowed for that again. "How can you just lie there? You have to get ready too."

"You're right," I grunt and push myself up from the bed. "Although my getting ready is a little less high maintenance."

Dana stops and puts her hands on her hips, glaring at me. "Are you calling me high maintenance?"

I can't help but smile. How have we already fallen into this sort of domestic bliss? Giving each other shit while walking around completely naked as if we've done this a million times before? "You're so cute when you're annoyed by me."

Her glare turns into surprise. "D-don't distract me." Dana continues shuffling through her clothes.

"I could say the same to you." I walk up behind her and

wrap my arms around her naked waist, pressing a line of kisses down her neck. "How can I look away when you're standing here looking so...fucking...alluring..."

The tension in her body melts, her head dipping back on my chest. "Drew...No time."

As I look down into her flushed face, I get the impulse to tell her what I've done. This stupid lie I've told.

"What is it?" she asks, reaching up to stroke my cheek.

I bite my lower lip. Not now. After. In bed tonight. When I can explain everything to her and tell her that we might as well make it real because of how badly I want her. "Nothing. Just gorgeous. You. You're gorgeous."

Dana pushes my chest playfully and I back off. "Let me get dressed, huh?"

I leave her to her sprint of a routine while I slowly slide on an army green linen shirt with cream-colored pants.

Dana is at the door with a minute to spare. "You're a modern marvel," I say, and I mean it. She went from completely naked to dressed, made up, and styled in a matter of nineteen minutes. And, while she'd look amazing to me in a paper bag, she looks even better in this orange and white patterned set of a floor-length skirt and crop top.

I go to open the door, but before I do, Dana catches me in a kiss. Sensual and divine. I touch her waist. The small, exposed line of her midriff drives me fucking wild. When we break apart, she smirks. "More of that later if you're good, huh?"

I hesitate. If only she knew how good I have already been, I don't know if she'd be singing the same tune. "Yeah. Sure," I say awkwardly before I open the door wide and our charade, the one Dana doesn't even know about, begins.

9

———

DANA

Sex ruins friendships. I knew this when I decided to cross that line with Drew. But from the way he responded to me, went wild for me, I thought we'd be okay.

Now, though, I'm not so sure.

We're sitting across from each other at a long banquet table in the hotel's main restaurant. Garlands of tropical flowers hang from the ceiling and everything is lit low, mostly with candles. Gillian and Axel sit together at the head of the table with Stella between them on a loveseat.

The rehearsal dinner is just for family and the bridal party, except everyone has a plus one (or two), so it's quite an event. All the children are excitedly snacking on fancy-looking grilled cheese while the adults gorge on delicious Maldivian delicacies.

I've just polished off the entirety of my banana flower salad (or Boshi Mashuni, as Hunter explained it's called). A delicious, aromatic mix of banana flowers and coconut. I glance around and realize most everyone is still eating theirs.

"You want some more?" Drew asks, holding up his plate.

I flush. "I should hold off to have room for the main course."

He shrugs. "I'm not going to eat it. You know how I feel about coconut."

"You shouldn't have come to Maldives, then," Hunter says with a waggle of his eyebrows.

"Had to. Comes with job," Drew replies.

I roll my eyes. "I am not a job."

"No, you're not. I'm teasing," he adds in a soft voice. "Take it."

I accept the plate and put it between Hunter and myself. "You'll help me eat this."

"Happy to."

I go to look back at Drew with thanks, but his attention is directed elsewhere. Down the table just a few rows. I swear he's looking at Willow. My stomach drops slightly.

I've heard stories about their relationship. I mean, it was so many years ago now. Almost five. But I know how heartbreak can be. From my understanding, Drew really left Willow with a broken heart. Not because he was intentionally cruel. What they say is true: when a heart breaks, it's never even. Willow just happened to be on the receiving end of a breakup, catalyzed by the death of Drew's mother.

I thought he was over her. But the way he's looking at her right now leads me to believe otherwise. Is he afraid that she can smell the sex on us. Make her jealous? Push her away?

Something feels off. Like he's not telling me something. It seemed like there was something on the tip of his tongue earlier when we were getting dressed. But he bit back on it.

Now I'm itching to know what might have come out of his mouth.

Maybe then I wouldn't feel so on edge.

Kira taps on my shoulder. "What's wrong?"

I force my mouth into a smile. I've gotten good at this habit and consequently, I don't think anyone can ever tell when I'm faking it. My sisters needed it when Mom left. "Nothing."

Kira purses her lips and narrows her eyes, gaze flipping between Drew and me. "You two are ridiculous, you know?"

I screw my face up. "What are you talking about?"

My sister digs her fork into her salad. "Don't act like you're slick."

I pull on the neck of my dress. Can everyone see that I, Dana Solace, have just had sex? Is it obvious to the naked eye? Is it because my hair is a bit unruly right now? I ran my hands through it in the mirror. I thought that–

Another tap, this time to my other shoulder. "Dana–"

The wedding planner, Bernice. I try not to audibly sigh. There's a reason Bernice is the best in the business, and it's because she's incredibly fastidious. Unfortunately for me, that means constant micromanagement. "Is something the matter?"

Bernice shakes her head, her blunt bob shuffling furiously side to side. "I'm sorry to interrupt you during the rehearsal dinner. I just wanted to address a change with you for the ceremony."

"Okay..." I say.

Bernice smiles appreciatively and then starts to walk away from the table.

"I think she wants you to follow her," Kira says unsurely in my ear.

I take my napkin out of my lap and throw it down on the table. "*Great.*"

Before I follow Bernice, I turn around swiftly and point at Hunter who has already scooped a portion of the salad onto his plate. "You better leave some of that for me!"

He freezes mid-motion. Little Jessica chortles while Amy scolds him.

With a laugh, I follow Bernice out of the restaurant.

***

"Do you want to try it one more time?" Bernice asks.

I shake my head.

"Okay, I know it's different than what we did in rehearsal, but–"

"Bernice, relax. It's just a different entrance point. I think we'll be okay."

Bernice the wedding planner interrupted me at my sister's rehearsal dinner simply to show me that instead of coming down the right side of the boardwalk, we'd now be entering from the left.

"I know, I know. I just–someone needs to be on top of this. I didn't want to interrupt your father, he looked too preoccupied."

I smile to myself. Aside from being the doting father we all know and love, trying to lavish Gillian with attention, he's also been a bit distracted by Victoria Neville who ended up leaving a photoshoot in Bali early to be able to make it tonight instead of early tomorrow morning.

He's been moon-eyed ever since and all of us know it, even Grant. We're all just waiting to see who will break first.

If I wasn't so sure that something weird was now up with Drew, I'd say that story sounded familiar.

"That was good of you. I'll make sure to keep him updated on the directions and everything tomorrow." Gillian has given me the express honor of accompanying her down the aisle with Dad. I cried when she told me.

Bernice sighs. "Well, alright, if you're sure you don't need to do it again—"

"I'm good," I say, maybe a bit too forcefully. How many times can she watch me slow-walk down the boardwalk without even Gillian next to me for practice? "Listen, Bernice," I say, subtly touching her arm to direct us both back toward the restaurant. "Have you even sat down the past few hours?"

"Sit down? You think I have time to sit down?"

"At least have a drink. The Maldivian Sunset is practically like juice," I explain as we get to the door of the restaurant. "You can't even taste the tequila."

Bernice's eyes widen. "Sounds dangerous."

I consider. "Now that you mention it..." I can feel the tequila starting to go to my head. I've already had two. Got to slow down.

"You're sweet, Dana, but I've got much too much to do before tomorrow. Which reminds me..." she trails off, finger to her lips.

I wait with bated breath for her to finish her sentence. However, Bernice just walks off in the opposite direction, clearly intent on whatever is next on her to-do list.

If I ever complain about my job, remind me it's nothing compared to the anxiety of being a wedding planner?

I turn to go into the restaurant and nearly run smack into someone. I jump out of my skin with surprise and clutch my chest. "Oh, my god!"

"Sorry. Did I scare you?"

If the near-collision didn't scare me, the pinched Valley girl tone of voice certainly did. "Willow...sorry, I didn't mean to get in your way. I just—"

"Not in my way at all. In fact, you were the person I was looking for."

I blink. "Oh?"

"I need to talk to you."

I shake my head. What the hell is happening? "About...?"

"About Drew, of course."

Of course. I touch the back of my head errantly. There must be some huge knot of hair unbrushed at the back there that makes it obvious I was bouncing in the sheets before I got here. "Um...what about?"

Willow huffs and rolls her eyes. She doesn't pretend to like me, and for that, I'm grateful. At all of the parties and showers leading up to the wedding, we remained rather cordial, keeping arm's length. Now, though, the truth is coming out.

I never understood why Gillian was friends with her anyway.

Willow's eyes are so wide that her long, ink-riddled lashes seem to tickle her eyebrows. "I think it's really shitty you never said anything about Drew all the times I've seen you the past couple months."

I stare at her. "About Drew?"

"Don't play the fool, Dana. Lord knows you and your sisters are good at that."

I don't mind Willow coming toe to toe with me. But to bring my sisters into it...that's the way to get me fired up. "I honestly don't know what you're talking about."

"You really are going to make me say it? That's fucking cruel."

"Willow, I don't know what the hell you're–"

"How long have you and Drew been together?"

What the fuck?

"We...I mean..."

"He told me on the trip over here. Made me look like an idiot too. I had no idea you two were..."

Her voice fades to the background as I get a creeping feeling over my skin. Someone is watching me. I carefully tilt my head to the side and look around her tall, pale shoulder. Drew is staring directly at us. And the look on his face...

Guilt.

That motherfucker.

"Hello! Earth to Dana, I'm talking to you."

My eyes snap right back into Willow's. "Sorry?"

Willow doesn't respond, just throws up her hands. *Well?*

Clearly, Drew lied to get her off his back. And Drew is my best friend. I'm not about to rat him out to his ex-girlfriend. However, just a couple of hours ago, my friendship with Drew turned into something totally different and way more complicated.

If I cover for him, I'm going down a dangerous road.

But I really don't think I have a choice.

"It's new," I say.

"He said you've been together *a while*."

What the fuck, Drew? He's seriously fucking painted me into a corner. When I get my hands on him... "You know Drew. A while to him is a drop in the bucket to anyone else," I say, throwing my hands up and forcing a smile.

Evidently, pretending we have a common ground

between her ex and my current "boyfriend" was not the right move. Willow straightens up her neck, making her as tall as a giraffe, and tosses her dark hair over her shoulders. "Well, best of luck. You'll need it."

She struts past me before I can say another word. I suck in my cheeks. Something tells me she's not wishing me luck because Drew's some toxic man who will never change. No, it felt much more...competitive than that.

I feel sick.

Too many Maldivian Sunsets.

I focus back on Drew. He's completely pale, negating any sort of tan he might have gotten today. And his mouth is ajar. He grips the back of his chair and starts to stand up.

But we're not going to do this now. This is Gillian's fucking rehearsal dinner and I'm not going to be the one to screw it up.

I shake my head and hurry back to the table. I again force my signature smile and grab the plate still half full with salad. "You listened!"

"Of course I did. You think I want to be on the bad side of Dana Solace? Think again?"

"Oh, I'm not *that* bad," I say, stabbing a piece of coconut with my fork. "Am I?"

Amy pops out from around Hunter's shoulder. "You don't get mad often, but when you do..."

I look at Drew. My smile slowly turns down, down, down...

"Let's just say I pray for whoever is on the other side of your fury."

Damn fucking right.

"Are you out of your fucking mind?" I yell at Drew the second the door to our bungalow is closed.

Drew doesn't respond, scratching at his chest like he has hives. "Is it hot in here or is it just me?" He goes off to the folding glass doors to let some air into the room.

"Don't fucking walk away from me."

"I'm not, I just need a second to...catch my breath," he says. He leans against the door and looks at the dark expanse of the sea. His deep breaths are audible. Deep breaths I taught him how to take in counseling.

I don't move a muscle as I wait for him to turn back around and be ready. I sat through all of dinner making small talk, indulging in toasts, *celebrating*. All the while my insides were burning.

Some might think a fake relationship might be a great foray into a real one.

To that, I say, fuck off.

If Drew wanted to be in a relationship with me, he should have asked. He's had one million opportunities over the past two years. In fact, I thought the reason he stopped using me as a counselor was because he saw me as more than that.

Nope. Two years of friendship.

Granted, I've told him on several occasions, I'm not really in a place to date. I've got too much on my mind between work, my family, and...

He was supposed to see between the lines. I don't have room to date. Unless it was him.

Fucking *idiot*.

Amy's right. I don't get mad a lot. But when I do, it's like everything that's bothered me for the past several months all compounds together to create a spew of lava from between my lips.

Sorry, Drew. You're going to get an earful tonight.

Drew finally turns around. "Could you turn on a light?"

"No."

He clenches his teeth nervously. "You're kind of scary in the dark."

"Drew. Explain."

"Okay, okay, fine." He brushes his hand back through his hair. Fuck that pretty, always appropriately messy hair. I'd love to run my fingers through it. In fact, that's what I thought we'd be doing after the rehearsal dinner tonight. We'd say our goodnights and goodbyes, the tension would build the whole walk back to the room, and *boom*, we'd be devouring each other once again.

I guess the tension did build the whole walk back to the room. Just not the way I wanted.

"Willow was coming onto me. Hard."

My anger flares again. This time, not at him. At myself. For how jealous I feel at the sound of Willow (or any woman) coming onto Drew.

"And you know all about that relationship. I mean, it was years ago now, I was a different person and–" He sighs. "I don't want that again. I don't want *her* again. Even if we've both changed. I mean, you get it, Dana, don't you?"

I do...I know all about their stories. They were that couple that met at a club who never had anything to talk about but had a lot of fun drinking together and fucking and being dramatic. Their three year relationship, when all was said and done, was really more like a year and a couple months between all the times they broke up.

Toxic. That's the word for her. Toxic.

But lying to her? Bringing me into it?

That's toxic too.

I've always known Drew was capable of that. In fact, in

the time I was his counselor, I watched him grow a lot from an immature guy fucking around in his twenties to a grown man trying to get and keep his shit together.

He's never been that way with me, though.

"Dana?"

Until now. "I understand why you did it, but..." I shake my head.

"You're upset. I know you're upset. That's fair. And I'm sorry. I'm really sorry I brought you into it without..."

Drew comes toward me. I don't have the strength to walk away. I still want him. He wraps his palms around my bare shoulders, a zip of electricity shooting through me. More pain than pleasure. "Look, what happened earlier had nothing to do with–"

"I know it didn't," I interrupt. I initiated it. That would have been a maniacal maneuver on his part to trick me into a relationship just to fulfill a lie. I can't deny it hurts, though. "I feel used, Drew."

"I didn't mean to–"

"You *know* it doesn't matter what you meant." I draw my arms up across my chest.

His hands fall from my shoulders and he looks away. "Right."

Neither of us speaks for a while.

"I know it would be a lot to ask you to continue lying for me..."

"There's a but, isn't there?"

Drew smiles. A pathetic, cute little half-smile. I wish I didn't like his face so much. "Would you just keep it up with me for the duration of the trip?"

My stomach falls. That's a long fucking time. Willow's staying the whole trip. It's not just a few days and then, presto chango, no relationship. It's two weeks of pretending.

On the other hand, though, I don't want to even imagine what kind of havoc Willow may wreak if she finds out Drew and I lied to her. Who knows what kind of drama would ensue?

Even worse, I know she would throw herself right back at him.

And I don't know how strong he'd be to resist. I may be mad at him, but I don't want that for him. Or for me.

"Fine," I say definitively and walk past him to get to the bathroom.

"Really?" he asks after me. I can hear the wide smile on his face.

"Really."

I sort through my clothes and grab some pajamas.

Drew follows me, his footsteps coming up behind me. "I owe you. I owe you big time."

"Yeah, you do."

"Seriously, Dana..." Drew brushes my hair off my shoulder. He leans down and kisses it.

I can't do this.

"Thank you," he whispers and presses his face to the side of my head.

Part of me wants him. Badly. The other part feels sick at his touch. "If we're going to do this, we can't do *this*," I say, pushing him away. "We do what we need to do in public to keep up appearances, but this—"

Drew frowns. "Why?"

"Because..." Because the truth is, if we pretend in public and in private, I'll fall even more in love with him. And it will all have been a lie. "Because you don't deserve it."

Drew laughs despite himself, then runs his hand over his mouth. I hear the light bristles of his facial hair against his skin. "Okay. Um. Fair."

I nod. "Yes. More than."

He nods harder. "Yes. More than."

God, this is just going to be a fucking echo chamber if I keep talking. I go to the bathroom, but before I can close the door, Drew calls after me. "Dana?"

"What?" I can't hide the rigid frustration in my voice.

But when his blue eyes meet mine...I can't stay mad. "Thank you. Seriously. You're the best."

I don't know what to say. So, I don't say anything and shut the bathroom door.

10

DREW

I knew it would be hard to feel in the Christmas spirit in Maldives. However, I don't even feel in a wedding spirit this Christmas Eve. My suit feels itchy. I can't help but feel like a child sitting through a parent teacher conference while the wedding processional begins.

I'm sitting next to Victoria Neville, a literal supermodel, whose face I saw on billboards for years. When I met her at a Solace family barbecue, I realized that *yes* some people are just that flawless in person. Dana used to tease me for the way I looked at her, but Victoria was just a convenient excuse not to look at Dana the way I really felt about her.

Victoria's niece, Tana, sits in her lap. Grant and Harley's daughter is a little young yet to be included in a wedding to do.

"Tissue?" Victoria asks, holding out a box toward me. Tana reaches her chubby hand out after the box.

I take one just to be polite. I can tell Victoria needs them. She started crying the second the processional started. Willow and one of Axel's college mates were the first to enter, followed by Amy and Hunter, then Grant and Harley. Tana called out after them, waving her hands in the air excitedly. That's what really brought on the waterworks.

I, on the other hand, have been staring straight ahead, my eyes idling on Axel's folded hands. I watch his thumbs circle each other, worrying. It's funny how everyone gets cold feet before a wedding. No matter how sure we are made to feel, humans don't trust each other in the end, do they?

That's grim. I'm feeling a bit...down, I guess.

Yesterday went from the best day of my life to one of the worst. All it took was one dinner and an idiotic lie to make Dana Solace absolutely disgusted with me. She even put a line of pillows between us in bed so we couldn't accidentally touch in the night.

Longest night of my fucking life. Especially when I'd been looking forward to waking up with her in my arms.

Victoria shakes my shoulder. "Drew. Up."

I come back to reality and realize the music has shifted and everyone is starting to stand for the bride. Damn, I missed Stella's big moment as the flower girl. I'm never going to forgive myself for that.

I get to my feet and straighten out my jacket. I'm wearing the lightest fabric possible, yet the Maldivian twilight is still making me sweat bullets.

"Oh, look at them," Victoria whispers. I can just hear more tears coming on.

I dare myself to look back at the end of the boardwalk. And I'm immediately grateful to have a tissue in my hand.

Yes, Gillian looks beautiful, that's a given. Every bride looks beautiful on their wedding day, that's nothing special.

It's Dana who captures my attention. All of the bridesmaids are dressed in a vibrant yellow, but Dana stands out in fiery orange. The dress dips down to the center of her chest, giving just a glimpse of her cleavage, and the skirt splits high up on her thigh.

None of that matters, though. It's her smile that makes her so beautiful. Beaming ear to ear, glossy lips, sparkling eyes. Proud to be on her sister's arm. As she should be.

My eyes fill with tears.

Every guest holds their breath as Gillian walks down the aisle, flanked by Kent and Dana. An orchestral version of a Frank Sinatra song accompanies them.

"Oh, Drew," Victoria says, glancing back at me. "Don't forget your tissue."

"I'm fine, I'm..." I'm not going to cry. That's pathetic. Depressing.

I just can't shake away the image of Dana walking down the aisle toward me someday. God. I want that.

As the trio passes our row, Dana remains steadfast in her mission to bear Gillian to Axel. Kent, on the other hand, becomes distracted by baby Tana gurgling for him. He blows her a quick kiss. Victoria bounces Tana on her hip.

Once they reach Axel under a canopy of flowers, I know all hope of being strong is lost for me. Gillian goes first to Dana, wrapping her arms around her older sister. I have a perfect view of Dana's face from here. And that bold smile, that confidence, all breaks at once. Tears start to stream down her cheeks. "It hasn't even started and I'm crying," I swear I hear her whisper.

Gillian laughs. Then, it's Kent's turn to give her away.

Dana steps into the line of bridesmaids, between Kira and Lola, and takes a deep breath.

You got this, D.

Her eyes find mine.

Shit, did she hear me?

And, thankfully, she smiles.

I smile back.

She wipes at her cheek.

I mirror her. And without realizing it, I'd let a tear escape.

"Please be seated."

"I GUESS you should hold my hand or something," Dana says.

We're standing awkwardly together at a tall table, both holding cocktails and sipping them in order to avoid speaking.

"Do you want me to hold your hand?"

Dana shrugs.

Great, that makes me feel just great. "Let's just be natural."

"How can we be natural in a situation like this?" Dana asks.

I sigh. From the second she walked in, things have been off. I tried to keep things light and easy by complimenting her dress, but she immediately flushed and changed the topic of conversation. Wrong move on my part, clearly.

One of the cater waiters walks by and I stop them for a spoonful of poke. I slide it into my mouth, realizing the fact I'm preoccupied and don't have to talk.

"So, my sisters know."

I nearly spit out my tuna. "What?" I ask.

"Don't talk with your mouth full," she admonishes the same way she does one of her nieces.

Great, so she hates me *and* I'm like a child to her. I

gulp the fish down in one go, trying not to think about how expensive that bite might have been. "You *told* them?"

"Don't act so surprised," Dana says. She pushes a cocktail straw into her Maldivian Sunset, a curl of hair falling over one eye. "Kira said she already knew."

I sigh. "I had to tell her. She was on my plane."

"Then don't be so surprised!" Dana retorts. "If one sister knows, the rest will follow. You know this."

Yes, I know this. "You didn't tell them that we—"

"Are you kidding?" she whispers tersely. "No fucking way."

I laugh without laughing. "Right, that would be embarrassing."

Dana cocks her head to the side. "Drew, you know I can't tell them about that. It has nothing to do with it being embarrassing."

I lean in slightly. She doesn't back away. "What does it have to do with, then?"

"Don't play dumb."

"I'm not. I want to know why your sisters can't know that we—"

Dana points her finger in my face. "Don't say it."

This is too fun. "Relax. I wasn't going to say fucked."

She throws her hand up. "Great. Glad you didn't say it."

"I was *going* to say 'boinked.'"

Dana does a double take. I can see the beginnings of a smile on her lips.

"You can laugh," I say. "I am funny."

"You're impossible. Not funny. There's a difference."

"Would you laugh if I said we 'bumped uglies' instead?"

"No."

"Dipped the wick?"

Dana opens her mouth, unable to contain her upturned lips. "*Drew.*"

"Took the skin boat to tuna town?"

That gets her. She descends into giggles, cheeks flushing pink. "You're ridiculous."

"Just want to know how you'd describe it."

"Where the heck did you learn *that?*" She holds up a hand, stopping me before I reply. "Actually, I don't want to know. But for the record, it is *not* tuna town down there."

I gulp, remembering the tuna sitting in my stomach.

Axel and Gillian approach our table. "The happy couple!" Axel announces.

"Is that meant to be irony?" I ask.

Gillian puts her hand on my shoulder. "We heard all about your little plan."

"Seems like an awful lot of work for one person, don't you think?" Axel asks, taking a sip of his whisky.

"It's not just Willow. It's also everyone else not in the family."

"Wait, *the family* knows?" I ask.

Dana rolls her eyes. "If one Solace sister knows, they all follow. And now that there are boyfriends–"

"Husbands!" Axel says. He wraps his arm around Gillian's waist and beams. "Husbands, actually."

"*Husbands,*" Dana acknowledges. "You know, it's all on a need to know basis."

"Except it seems like everyone needs to know," I reply with an eyebrow raised.

Dana smiles, although there's no happiness in it. "You're the one who decided to lie to your ex-girlfriend that we're a couple at my sister's wedding, so–"

"Well, your sister is the one who decided to put my ex-girlfriend in the wedding party," I reply.

"Which, for the record, I regret," Gillian says. "She's been nothing but a pain in the–"

She's interrupted by the searing squeak of mic feedback. We all turn toward a stage that's been setup at the back of the cabana. Grant is standing at a mic, waiting for it to calm down. "Good evening, everyone. I hope you're enjoying celebrating the happy couple."

Gillian and Axel nuzzle together and exchange a look of what can only be described as love and makes me desperately miserable.

"Gillian, I've known you longer than I think any of us would like to talk about, and it's been an honor being in your life and officially part of the family. And Axel, welcome to the Solace fold. I know it's overwhelming, but you'll catch on faster than you think."

The room laughs politely.

Dana subtly moves toward me, bobbing her shoulder. *What?*

"I could stand up here and give a whole speech, or I could just get to the point of why I've interrupted cocktail hour."

"Wrap your arm around me, doofus," Dana whispers.

I do it faster than she can blink an eye. With her tucked under my arm. I feel like we must look just as good as Axel and Gillian do.

"So, as a wedding gift..."

I glance around the room to see if we're being clocked. Most everyone is staring at Grant, waiting for him to get off the stage. Except one person.

You can probably guess who.

Willow's eyes are like ice on my skin.

I ignore her and instead trace my thumb across the skin

of Dana's shoulder. She glances at me but doesn't tell me to stop.

Grant clears his throat. "I'd like to welcome, Hanna Call and the Strangers to the stage."

That's a jumble of words I don't even know what to do with. However, from Gillian's reaction, I can tell it's a big deal.

"What?!" she screams. "No!"

Axel grins.

"Did you–"

"Grant's idea, I swear!"

The two lovebirds head off toward the stage where a scraggly group of musicians are assembling. "Who..."

"Hanna Call and the Strangers," Dana repeats. "Gillian's favorite band. They're from LA, actually, and she's been a fan ever since before they were big."

I've never heard of them, but I guess that just means I'm getting old, not that they aren't big.

"Infinium opened up a record label and they're one of the first groups they signed," Dana continues.

Grant's company, Infinium, seems to have their hands in everything these days. "Wow."

Dana chews on her lower lip. "You don't have to keep your arm around me. If you don't want to."

I look at my hand on her sun-kissed skin. "What if I want to?"

A small smile creeps across her lips and she rolls her eyes. But she doesn't tell me to stop. So, I don't.

This is going to be a long vacation if we're playing this game.

"Good evening, everyone!" a woman shouts into the microphone. "I'm Hanna and these are the Strangers. We're so happy to be here tonight to bring music to Gillian and

Axel's big day. We'll start out with one you might know pretty well."

The woman starts to strum on a guitar that looks like something Carl Perkins would have played. It's a slower song. And I instantly recognize it. It's one of those songs I never knew, but just *knew*.

The singer, Hanna, purrs into the microphone, a gravely, sultry song. It has all those buzzwords in love songs. Want. Hunger. Desire.

Fuck.

Dana and I stand stock straight for a while just watching. Gillian and Axel begin to dance, Gillian singing along to every word. Other couples begin to migrate over and join them.

"Should we..." she begins.

"I thought you'd never ask." I grab her hand and drag her onto the dance floor.

———

ONE DANCE TURNS INTO TWO, turns into I don't know how many. Even after we all have to break for dinner, we're immediately back on our feet. It's easier that way. The point of me being here was to have fun with my best friend. Things might be a little complicated (I know, an understatement), but we can still enjoy each other's company.

Late in the night, Hanna Call and the Strangers take their leave and we're left with a quintessential wedding DJ with dark sunglasses and a backwards baseball cap. We jam to all the wedding classics, including "Dancing Queen" and "Sweet Caroline".

Then, the DJ throws on the Electric Slide and Dana freezes up.

"What? Why are you stopping?" I ask between heaving breaths. Somehow, I've forgotten about the tropical heat despite the sweat pouring down my face.

"I don't know this one!" she shouts over the music.

"What?! You don't know 'The Electric Slide'?"

Dana shakes her head. Her updo has fallen out almost completely and her makeup isn't nearly as perfect as it was earlier, but man, is she gorgeous.

"It's a classic."

"To whom?"

I roll my eyes. "Come on, I'm not that much older than you."

"Old enough," she grins.

I feel a swell of excitement in my belly. Five years isn't much...enough to make me feel like I can take care of her. "I'll teach you. Come on."

I take her hand without thinking what it might mean.

"Just watch and try and copy!" I cry out.

I grapevine to the right, stop and stomp. Dana jerks to stop after me.

"It's okay, you'll get it."

Grapevine the other way, stop and stomp. She gets it this time.

"Yes!"

I walk her through the rest of the dance. There are others watching me and picking it up themselves. And eventually, by the fourth go of it, Dana doesn't need my hand to guide her. She's got it all on her own.

"It's electric!" I shout along with the music.

"Boogie-woogie-woogie!" she calls afterward.

Kent sidles up to me, dancing along to the music a little off-beat. "Ah, my favorite couple! Dancing my favorite dance!"

"*Dad*, don't be so obvious," Dana scolds.

Great. *All* the Solaces know.

And if all the Solaces know, then it's only a matter of time before they start trying to shoehorn this fake relationship into a real one.

Maybe it's wrong of me, but there's no way in hell I'm going to stop them.

11

———

DANA

When I get out of bed, it hurts to put my feet on the floor.

"Ah! Shit!"

"Mmgh. What is it?" Drew grunts, his voice muzzled by what sounds to be a pillow.

I try again, softer this time. There are blisters all over my feet from my strappy shoes, and my calves are so sore I feel like they're about to lock up. "Nothing. It's fine. Go back to bed."

"No, I'm up. It's Christmas, after all."

I glance back at Drew from rubbing my calves. He's pushed himself halfway up out of bed, hair all mussed and pushed in different direction, eyes squinting in the morning sun.

Man, the things I would do to this man.

"Um, just my calves. All the dancing." I push myself up from the bed. Have to get away from him so I don't do anything stupid. The bottoms of my feet ache, zinging pain up to my knees. "A-a-and my feet. Fuck."

"You want me to rub them?"

I turn toward him as slowly as someone would toward a strange sound in a horror movie.

"Sorry, is that weird?" he asks with one eyebrow popping upward.

"Yeah. Rubbing my feet as my not-boyfriend would be weird, Drew."

He shrugs. I admire how resilient he is. I am admittedly being a bit of a jerk, especially after how much fun we had last night. "When do we have to be in the suite?"

"Brunch is at ten."

Drew glances at the clock on the nightstand, red number blaring the numbers eight and zero and two. "I'm going back to sleep, then." He collapses back into the mountain region of pillows just north of the sea of blankets.

I sigh, thinking how nice it would be to crawl in next to him. Push my face into his neck. Inhale deeply.

In another life maybe. Right now, I've got to shower and figure out what to do about these blisters.

Axel and Gillian are probably the most masochistic newlyweds of all time. Their bridal suite is overrun with the entire Solace-and-friends crew in order to celebrate our tropical Christmas. Hunter even had the suite decorated to the nines for the occasion. For a family holiday abroad, you would think we just stepped out of a catalog for Christmas.

The only difference, of course, is no one is indulging in hot beverages or sitting by a fire. Even though LA never gets frigid, we still get to indulge in the cooler side of the weather by Christmas. Here it's just hot. And sweaty.

In true spirit of "hair of the dog," all the adults are fisting a mimosa while the children sit around the

Christmas tree tearing open presents. Getting those back to LA sounds like a logistical nightmare and, thankfully, is not my problem.

"I've almost got it…"

Drew has become the master of the toys that require batteries. He's using his engineering degree to the fullest, running around and using a tiny screwdriver to open up ports and plug in batteries.

He's currently trying to open the bottom of Jessica's remote-controlled Barbie car. His tongue is resting in the corner of his mouth as he spins the screwdriver around and round until–

"Yes, got it!" The bottom of the car unlocks and opens up a battery compartment. He eyes the screw. "Thing was stripped."

"What's that mean?" Jessica asks.

"Well, do you see how this screw has ridges and this one doesn't?" Drew launches into a long-winded explanation of what makes a screw stripped. Jessica is trying to pay attention as best she can, but he might have lost her when he started the history of the screw part of the lesson.

I smile. I can't help it. He's got a way with the kids. It's not the way you would usually think, the guys who come barreling in and run around with the kids until they're all tuckered out. Not the Uncle Drew that they clamor for at the door.

His talent is much more understated. He takes time with them. Even with Tana, he's methodical in the way he speaks to her. The first time he held her, he frowned and said, "You'll understand me when you're older."

"You've got yourself in it now, haven't you, littles?" Dad rumbles in my ear.

I chuckle. "Littles" has been his name for me since I was

a baby. I'm the oldest, probably should be called "bigs", but I've always been "littles." Dad always says it's because one is the tiniest number.

It's also the loneliest.

"Why are you getting on my case about this too?" I ask. Dad had to be looped in. Obviously. If he saw Drew and me pretending to be a couple out of nowhere, I think he'd shout something to the likes of, "All my prayers have been answered." Not that Dad is a praying man.

He shakes his head. "It's just funny, isn't it? I mean, the way you two act around each other is…"

The motor of the car goes off, wheezing. Jessica claps excitedly while Drew holds it up in the air as if he's won some sort of trophy. He looks to me for approval. It's endearing, and also almost sad at this point. "How about that?"

"Nice one, bud," I say with a thumbs up.

Dad grimaces. "I was going to say natural, but that was—"

"Look, I'm doing him a favor. That's all."

"Yes, but sometimes a favor can turn into more. Keep yourself open to it. That's all I want, Dana. If you and Drew *actually*—"

I see Willow out of the corner of my eye scrolling on her phone. She walked into the suite late and slung herself into an easy chair and I haven't seen her move, an alligator lying in wait. "Lower your voice, Dad."

He follows my gaze.

"Don't look, don't—"

And of course that's the moment Willow looks up. She grins and gives us a little wave, twiddling her fingers.

"Dammit, Dad."

"Sorry, I was confused. You can't blame me for being confused."

I grab his arm. I want to say something scathing, but I don't. I never do. Rarely to my sisters. Never to my dad. I take a deep breath. "It's fine. No big deal."

Willow pushes herself up from her spot and goes to the breakfast buffet, humming to herself. It's eerie.

"Well, I think I've done my duty," Drew says, scanning the room. For only two children, Stella and Jessica have made quite the mess. Tana opened presents too, but it was more Grant unwrapping them and showing them to her while Harley bounced her on her knee and cooed about how wonderful *The Very Hungry Caterpillar* was.

Drew comes and sits next to me. He lifts his hand and hesitantly puts it on my knee. "Too much?" he whispers.

I look around. The people who know this is a lie greatly outnumber those who don't.

But I'm not going to tell him to stop touching me.

"It's fine," I say with a smile.

For a moment, our eyes lock. It feels like his body is undulating closer, imperceptible to the human eye. Like he might kiss me.

"So, you two must be next, huh?" Willow's razor sharp voice cuts through the moment.

I duck my head down, away from Drew. "What do you mean?"

She smiles sneakily. "You know..." Shimmying her shoulders, her somehow perfectly wavy hair swirls side to side. "Love, marriage, baby carriage."

"Oh!" Drew gasps. "Well–"

"You know, we're–" I look at him.

"Yeah, we're–"

"Not in a rush," I say at the exact moment he says, "No rush."

His hand tightens on my knee. If I wasn't in a rush a moment ago, I might be now.

"That's such a diplomatic answer," Willow says, popping a grape into her mouth. "What do you think, Mr. Solace?"

Shit.

"M-me?" Dad says, pointing to himself like bad actor in a play.

My father is a horrible liar which is why most of us knew Santa wasn't real by our fifth birthdays.

"Yeah! You've got three of them all wifed up. Or nearly." Willow nods toward Amy and Hunter who are standing near the tree, clearly exchanging some sort of sentimental gift. Why do I have to miss out on the beautiful moments to deal with a problem Drew created for me? "So, you must be excited Dana might be next. Your eldest, after all."

Dad maniacally smiles at me, almost all gums. *Jesus, Dad. This is rough.* "I just want them to be happy."

"Yeah, but tik tock, you know?"

I stare at Willow. "I'm only thirty."

"Oh really? Thought you were older." Another grape.

"Hey, Willow. Sometimes you say things and they're... rude," Drew intercedes, moving his hand from my leg to the couch behind me. Thank god.

Her big eyes widen even more. "I didn't mean for that to be rude. Sorry. It was just...Forgive me, Dana. I just thought you were like thirty-five or something."

I'm already thinking about my fast-approaching birthday. Not sure why Willow feels the need to make it worse. Other than the fact she's just being a jerk.

"I'm going to–I need another–" Dad holds up his still half-full mimosa.

"Yeah, that's a great idea," I say, practically pushing him off the couch.

Willow swoops in just a little closer. "So, Drew. Did you ever decide on the kid thing?"

I feel Drew tense beside me.

"He was always so unsure, you know?" Willow says, taking a seat on the arm of the couch. "Then again, we were so young. At least I was." She traces a finger through the fine leather. "Men have it so easy. I mean, look at Mick Jagger."

"You know, Willow. I really appreciate the question, and I'm afraid I just don't think we owe you an answer," I say. Diplomatically, of course.

Willow tilts her chin down. "I always thought you were nice, Dana."

"I am plenty nice," I reply, *for those who deserve it.*

I feel Drew brush a knuckle against my shoulder encouragingly.

"Fine." Willow scans the room for the next conversation she can enter unprompted. "Be careful, though. That not rushing thing might bite you in the end. Drew might spend his whole life not rushing." Her eyes zero in on Gillian and Axel, eager to be their third wheel. "Anyway..."

When she's just out of earshot, I let out a deep breath.

"Way to go, D, way to go!" Drew says, patting my shoulder.

"God, I really don't like her."

"You can say hate, I won't tell anyone."

I give him a look. "I don't hate anyone."

"Right. Not in the job description, hm?"

We smile at each other, and again I feel that pull, the

one that was happening before we were rudely interrupted. Willow isn't done with us, at least not with her evil little glare. I'll fucking show her. I give into the pull, dodging Drew's lips at the very last minute and planting a kiss to his cheek. Prolonged. Tender. A fuck you to Willow. And a little something for me too.

"What's that for?" Drew asks, his question a mere hot breath in my ear.

"For sticking up for me," I reply. "And to see the look on Willow's face."

He laughs lightly. "You're the best, D."

I want another kiss. On the lips this time. But I can't. Would be too much...wouldn't be fair to either of us. And besides, I made the line very clear. No funny business. All of it for the sole purpose of making Willow back off.

When he calls me the best, though...a whole colony of butterflies erupts in my belly.

I have to squash each and every one.

I pull away. "What are friends for?" I ignore any reaction he might have and eye Amy and Hunter across the room, the two of them now blissed out on the couch, watching Jessica dress her Barbie and stick her into her new car. Amy's got a new necklace on. Something simple but clearly expensive. Jewelry. That's a gift I'd like from a man. I'm not too proud to admit it.

"I got you something," Drew whispers.

"Huh? We agreed we wouldn't–"

"Little something. *Little.*"

Drew reaches into his pocket and pulls out a silver-foiled pack of baseball cards. The branding on the front is clearly vintage. I grin and take it. "That's not little. That might contain a–"

"Nineteen-fifty-two Mickey Mantle," Drew says with

me in unison. "Yeah, doubt that. But anyway. Merry Christmas, D."

I bite my lower lip. "I got you something too."

"And you were ready to give me shit about my thing!"

"It's just back in LA. I couldn't carry it." I'm lying. I didn't get him anything. Very unlike me. However, when Drew and I make pacts like that, I tend to stick to them. I'll have to think of something good in the meantime.

Drew blushes. "Well, thanks."

"Here, let's open them," I say. "You do the honors."

12

———

DREW

I can't take it anymore.

It's been over a week of pretending with Dana. Eleven days. Almost two full weeks.

Too much.

I have blue balls for romance. All this pretending has been like a long tease. Scratching that itch I've had for Dana for all this time.

Thankfully, since Christmas, everyday has been planned out almost to a "t" leaving barely any dead space for us to languish around the room, silently both stewing in how awkward this is. Fundamentally, things aren't awkward. Dana is still Dana. My best friend.

What's awkward is how much I have to think about what I'm feeling, about how much I feel about thinking about what I'm feeling. Sounds complicated, right?

To complicate matters even further, pretending is starting to feel real. When we're out with the group, which has dwindled from the original mass of guest to about thirty people, Dana and I just seem to turn on. Like a switch. We light up around each other, stopped asking if it's fine to touch each other, and come as a package deal in everything we do.

Now it's New Year's Eve. And everyone, and I mean everyone, will be expecting a kiss.

Because the Solace sisters are on my case to make this fake relationship a real one.

"If you want something more private, there's a perfect spot over in the grotto," Kira explains in my ear as I stare straight ahead through the throng of drunken partygoers. Hunter has commandeered the whole restaurant at the hotel and flown in other friends, so it's a real banger, not just people milling and seething, bored of each other's company.

"There's no way she'd go anywhere alone with me right now," I say, glancing down at my watch. Quarter to midnight.

"She knows that you have to have the midnight kiss to really clinch the deal. I'm sorry, but Willow is looking for any crack to steal you away," Kira explains.

"Yeah, which means a little peck under the fireworks where everyone can see. Not taking her somewhere private to—"

Kira makes a sound of a guinea pig being stepped on. "You're being difficult."

"You're trying to make something happen that's not going to happen, Kira Solace. Let's be clear about that."

She stomps her feet petulantly. "Drew!"

I laugh. "What!"

"I'm trying to help you. I'm trying to give you tips so you can make something happen with my sister."

"Kira! It's not going to happen."

"Why?!"

I swallow. I'm not going to dox Dana. She set a boundary and I'm respecting it. As much as I'd like it to change...I'm not going to rope her sisters into some sort of plot to get her to fall in love with me. I think that would just make it worse.

Kira grabs my arm, forcing me to look at her. "Dude. We're tired."

"Of..."

"This! You two pretending there isn't something between you when there very clearly is. You literally light up around each other. You're *perfect* for each other. Even in the way you're both too stubborn to admit it."

She might be ripping me to shreds, but hearing that Dana lights up around me makes me smile.

"And now you have that dopey grin on your face." She grabs me by the shoulders. "Find her. Go give her a kiss at midnight. Alone, huh?"

I simply smile.

Kira drops her hands and rolls her eyes. "A lost cause, that's what you are."

"You've done what you can. Now go have some fun," I say, nodding toward the party.

Kira gives me a sympathetic smile and leaves me with a pat on the arm before going to make her rounds.

I'd like nothing more than to kiss Dana at midnight. Not to make a show of it. But to really kiss her. Let her know exactly how I feel. It's my fault I'm in this mess. Who knows how this all would have shaken out if I hadn't told Willow that stupid lie. We could have had two weeks in paradise together. Seen if we could be a little bit more.

Okay, a lot bit more. I'd like everything with Dana if she'd let me.

The shuffling party goers seem to part ways before me, giving me a glimpse of the exact object of my thoughts and affection. Dana is swaying side to side, a drink in her hand (one of her favorites, those Maldivian Sunsets), while Amy talks to her at a mile a minute as Amy is wont to do.

She looks nice. Better than nice. But nice is the only word that feels polite to use to compliment her without it teetering into "I want more" territory.

Gorgeous is the word. Breathtaking.

She's wearing a black cropped shirt and silk shorts tied at the waist with a bow, and her hair is clipped back in a loose ponytail.

I feel like a slob compared to her. I've gone through all my linen shirts and suits, had them cleaned by the hotel too. But tonight I've opted for a simple short-sleeve button down patterned with watermelons. I brought it because she likes this one. Now, though, I feel like a clown.

"Ten minutes to midnight!" someone shrieks excitedly.

The energy in the room shifts, the bustle turning into hushed, excited conversation. I can only imagine it's everyone plotting out how wonderful their upcoming year is going to be. What great adventures they'll have with the love of their life.

I'm bitter. I'm bitter at people I care about. I used to feel that way when I saw people with their mothers in public. It felt like everyone was showing off their happy, healthy, living mother.

I need a breath of fresh air. If a fake kiss with Dana won't do for everyone, then what would be so bad about no kiss at all?

The party is all starting to gravitate toward the deck surrounding the restaurant that overlooks the water. I don't even want to think about how much money Hunter put into arranging a fireworks display for us.

I go the opposite direction, toward the boardwalk. I think I'll go back to the room. Turn in early. That way Dana doesn't even have to deal with me. I'll be in bed, on my side of the Great Wall of Pillows, which remains tall and firm, sleeping. And she doesn't have to even worry about my lips touching hers.

I shove my hands in my pockets as I walk down the dock, my sandals slapping hollowly. I'm in paradise and I've never felt worse.

I end up walking past our villa by accident, but then just keep walking on purpose. The boardwalk forms a loop where villas and cabins jut off in all directions, leaving a pool of sea water in the middle, like a lagoon. I've jogged around it a few times in the mornings. A walk will do me good.

I walk until I'm on the opposite side of the boardwalk, moseying down, until I spot some movement out of the corner of my eye. I look up and frown. Across the way, right in front of our cabin, is a silhouetted figure. It saunters up to the railing overlooking the central lagoon until it's...*she*'s bathed in light.

Dana.

"I was wondering how long it was going to take you to notice me," she calls out.

I lean on the railing. "What are you doing out here?"

"Coming to ask you what *you're* doing out here."

I laugh bashfully. "Oh, well. It was getting a little stuffy in there for me."

Dana tilts her head to the side. "You alright?"

"Yeah. Fine."

"Mm. Not convincing."

"Really, Dana, I'm–"

"You forget I know how to read you like a book," she interrupts. Though we're shouting across the lagoon, her voice doesn't sound strained.

I bite my lower lip. *I wish you didn't.*

Dana then follows the curved path of the boardwalk over to my side. My heartbeat quickens as she approaches.

"Good view of the fireworks over here, probably," she says, sidling over to the opposite railing.

I join her, leaving a healthy gap between us.

"Better than trying to elbow around for room over there," Dana adds, gesturing over in the direction of the restaurant, a mere blip in the distance.

I can't find the words to say what I'd like to. I'm just shocked she's left the safe confines of the party to come follow me.

"Now tell me," she says, leaning in slightly. "What's going on?"

"I'm just overwhelmed. I need a vacation from my vacation."

"Ew."

I laugh. "You asked."

"I still don't think you're telling me the whole truth..." she replies in a sing-song voice.

I shake my head. "No, I'm not."

Dana's forehead tightens.

"I don't think it'd be fair for me to burden you with all my feelings when they're–" *You're not fooling anyone, Drew. Just say it.* "When they're about you."

Though the restaurant is in the distance, the sound of people counting down from ten resounds clearly over the water.

Dana only looks at me, the corners of her eyes down-turned. She's pitying me.

I rest my elbows on the rail, feeling even more pathetic than before. "See? I told you. It's just not–"

"...two...one...*Happy New Year!*"

I look in the direction of the clamor. Without missing a beat, the fireworks begin, a sprig of gold shuddering through the air.

Despite the show erupting in the sky, Dana hasn't taken her eyes off me.

"Look, this has gotten really screwy. With all the pretending and everything. I'm a wreck trying to make sure I don't make things worse, touching you in public, barely able to speak to you in private. Meanwhile, your sisters are all giving me their two cents, and none of that matters, because I fucked everything up before anything could even begin, and the last thing I want to do is lose my best friend over something really stupid I said. So." I gesture to the sky as cherry-red sparks across the stars. "Happy New Y-"

I'm cut off by Dana's lips. On mine. Her arms link around my neck, drawing me close to her chest. I briefly wonder if she spotted someone and now she's just playing the part I set out for her. But when her tongue grazes the corner of my mouth, I know it's real. That extra little bit pushes me over the edge.

I slide my hands carefully onto the small of her back, pressing my entire self to her. Closer, closer, until I'm wound around her without an inch to spare.

Fireworks don't compare to what's happening inside me. The popping, sparking energy of having Dana close to me like this again. And it's real.

That must mean something, right?

I tear my lips away from hers. "Did your sisters tell you to do this?" I ask breathlessly.

"Why are you bringing my sisters up at a time like this?" she retorts and then kisses me before I can answer.

She's right. I don't care about an answer. Not when her fingers wrench around the front of my shirt and she yanks me toward her, so hard I stumble and have to catch myself on the railing.

"Shit, sorry," she says with a smile, her hand cupping the back of my neck.

"Don't be sorry. Never be sorry for that." In fact, I give in to the tumbling, frantic energy. I sweep Dana's hips into my mine, drawing her off-balance, causing us to cascade to the ground. I don't even have a chance to ask if she's alright before she digs her fingernails into my shoulder blades and presses her pelvis up against me.

"I've been trying..." she mutters between kisses. "I've been trying to be strong."

I run my hand down her leg, feeling the goosebumps on her thigh. The soft, buttery skin I've dreamed about every night makes the blood go straight to my head.

And another place, if I'm honest.

"But I can't do it anymore."

"Who said you had to be strong?" I say and then begin a trail of kisses down her jaw. "When have you ever had to be strong for me?"

"Because...because..." Dana doesn't finish, letting out a long moan.

The sound sends wildfire down my spine. "Dana, when you make sounds like that, I just...I have to have you."

Our faces linger merely an inch apart. Her breath is close, wet, hot. I want her tongue. I want her mouth. I want every part of her.

It doesn't matter to me that we're out on the boardwalk late in the night. It's like we're in our own cosmic universe, the fireworks blasting out in the distance, night sky wide above, sea ready to sweep us away.

Dana touches my cheek, sliding her thumb back and

forth against my chin. Her thighs clench around my hips. "Yeah."

I nearly snort with laughter. "Yeah?"

"I mean, yeah, that sounds good."

"For someone so eloquent–"

"How can I be eloquent when I'm horny?" she whispers back and starts to close the gap between us as if she'll kiss me.

I shake my head. "Don't have to be. Just giving you shit."

Lips on lips, she stops just shy of doing the deed. "I love when you give me shit."

I love everything about you. I don't dare say that aloud. That would be some sort of suicide.

Dana locks her elbow around my neck, kissing me harshly, her nose pressing hard into my face. My hips start to undulate into her. God, we're really doing this again. And we're doing it here. This is a dream come true. Every dream I've had in bed with her even though it felt like we were miles apart.

I can't wait to have her tonight.

A thumping distracts me. So loud it couldn't be my heart. I pull my lips off Dana's and look over my shoulder. "*Shit.*"

Though I can't make out the faces yet, I see a horde of people running down the boardwalk.

"Get up, get up, get up," Dana says, patting my chest hurriedly.

I roll off her and get onto my feet.

"Skinny dipping!" a voice shouts from the group, emerging proudly.

"Gillian, no," Dana says and rushes forward.

Gillian is already half-unclothed, the top of her dress draped over her hips and her bra still keeping her decent.

Axel is no better, following after her with his pants around one ankle and shirt flying open. They are accompanied by other familiar faces. Lola, Harley, Willow.

Dear god, Willow.

"Come with us, Dana!" Gillian says with a broad grin.

"Yippee!" Axel leaps into the lagoon, water splashing up onto us.

Dana recoils. "No, you're all drunk. You have no idea what could–"

"You into party poopers now, Drew?" Willow smirks and then dives into the water gracefully still in her underwear.

Dana turns to look at me for some sort of assistance.

And while I'd never make Dana do anything she didn't want to do... "Could be fun."

"You're kidding."

I pull my shirt over my head and toss it to the side. "No."

"That's the spirit! Come on, be like your *boyfriend!*" Harley teases, pulling on the button of Dana's shorts.

"Harley, no, no, *no!*"

Harley pulls too hard, sending them both tumbling into the lagoon.

"No fair, I was supposed to go first," Gillian balks and goes in after them.

I rush to the edge, scanning the water worriedly. Harley and Dana don't emerge. I unbuckle my belt and start to aggressively shake off my khakis. "Guys?!"

Suddenly, Dana and Harley both break through the water with a gasp. Dana spits out a stream of water. I'm ready for her to be irate, but instead, she looks at Harley and splashes her as hard as she can. Harley laughs and splashes back.

An all-out war starts in the water between all the skinny dippers. The fireworks still march on high, loud claps of manmade thunder.

"Hey, D!" Dana calls out to me. "Water's fine."

I smile at her, a sliver of disappointment in my chest. Wouldn't matter if we tried to reset. Moment's over anyway. I take a deep breath and dive in.

13

____

DANA

I open the door from my office to the waiting room and smile at Rita, my client. "Thanks for coming in today. I hope you got what you needed."

Rita smiles as she walks past me. "Always do, Dana."

I flush. It's a nice feeling to know I've helped people. It's what keeps me coming back to the job even though sometimes it can be quite the burden to walk people through grief.

Rita stops suddenly. "Well, these are nice."

I frown and peer around her. At the sign-in desk, there's a huge bouquet of flowers. Roses. Yellow.

"Those weren't here when I walked in, were they?" she asks. "You know my memory these days..."

"No, I can assure you they weren't." I slink past her and examine the flowers. A small envelope sticks out of the top.

Rita appears at my elbow, grinning excitedly. "Secret admirer?"

I pop the envelope open. "Not sure."

"Not-so-secret admirer? Even better!" Rita exclaims.

I slide the card out; before I even read the note, my eyes

flick to the signature. It's Drew's scraggly penmanship. My heart does a somersault. "Gosh, um..."

"I'll leave you to it," Rita says, tapping me softly on the arm and starts to go. "Same time next week?"

"Y-yes, of course," although I'm not really paying attention to what I'm saying. The words are swimming on the page. I have to concentrate to put them in order.

Dana,

Maybe I shouldn't be thinking about you, but I am.

Talk soon? Please?

Drew.

Okay, I may be actively avoiding Drew since we got back to the States. We needed some time apart. Give us time to take a breath and reset our friendship after pretending to be in a relationship for two weeks.

After our close encounter on the dock, things between us softened. Not entirely, but enough to bring down the wall of pillows in our bed.

I couldn't help it. That night, after skinny dipping, I couldn't seem to warm up. And Drew was there, with his broad chest and big hands. What, I was just going to say no to that? So, I removed two pillows from the top half of the fence and snuggled into his chest.

Drew accepted me into his arms without a word. No questions. No attempt at anything more. Just held me all night.

In the morning, we pretended like it didn't happen.

The same thing happened the final three days of our trip. Pretending in public we were lovers, pretending in private we weren't.

The mental gymnastics was exhausting.

We've exchanged a few texts since returning home. But

the past three weeks, I've avoided phone calls and invitations to hang out.

Hasn't stopped him from trying. In fact, this is the third bouquet of flowers he's sent me. One for each week I've been distant. And flowers aren't the only thing he's sent. He also sent me a double batch of his famous garbage cookies, the only thing he really knows how to bake. Cookies with anything in the pantry, at least anything that could reasonably go into cookies without someone turning their nose up at them.

I ate them all and didn't share. Something about stress does that.

I pull out my phone and snap a picture for Kira. She texts me back not even three seconds later with a line of expletives and then–

Just kiss already!

If only she knew we did a lot more than that in Maldives.

My sisters think I'm crazy for resisting his advances. Because that's what they are. He can say they're in the name of friendship (yellow roses! The friendship color! Yeah, right), say that it's just because he wants me back in his life as *friends*, but all of this is giving way more than friendship.

It's giving romance.

I'm so close to giving into it.

But something keeps holding me back.

I know Drew too well. He's become my best friend in the past two years. But before that, I was his counselor. Another two years where I got to know the deepest parts of him. He was ruthlessly honest and open. Which is good. That's how it should be.

The thing about grief counseling is that you don't just hear about a person's grief. You hear about their whole lives. Because grief doesn't live in some sort of vacuum. It affects everything just as it's affected by everything.

I was party to his relationship with Willow ending. Let me be clear, that relationship needed to end.

However, I also have heard him say some choice things about his ability to commit.

"Who is to say I'm even meant to be in a relationship? Meant for all that. Sounds like something in a fairy tale, if I'm honest."

I remember that day vividly. Three months in. He smiled that small, quintessential Drew smile. Tight and sneaky, yet utterly adorable. He must have been a hellion who all the teachers loved in school. But anyway, I remember that day because it was the first day my heart skipped a beat. Drew's an attractive guy, that's obvious. But just because a man is attractive doesn't mean you want to give yourself over to him.

That was the first moment I wanted to give myself over to Drew.

And it terrified me.

Because if he was afraid of his ability to commit, who is to say he would be any different than my own mother? My mother did the unthinkable, walking out on a husband and five children after almost twenty years of marriage. Of motherhood. And she washed her hands of us. Clean. We were all left with the dirt and wreckage of her disappearance.

I believe in the goodness of people. I've also seen the worst of them. And as much as I love Drew (platonically, right?), I fear he will leave. I've feared it through our friendship. I can only imagine that feeling would intensify if we got any closer.

Nearly four years of that feeling. It wears on a person.

My heart and head are both yelling at me, trying to be heard over the din. So, instead of making a decision on who's right, I've just frozen.

Another text from Kira comes in on my phone.

Did you thank him?

I chew on my upper lip. I've thanked him for everything, of course. I'm not a monster. But it's always been very, well, platonic. Something like. "Wow, thanks!" or "Drew, you shouldn't have."

Kira. Again.

You know he'd love to hear from you...

I mute our conversation and let out a sigh. She's right. However, I don't know what to say.

Tapping my phone in my hand, I pace back and forth. What would sufficiently communicate what I want to say? Hell, what do I even *want* to say?

I settle for something simple. *They're beautiful. I feel like I need to find a way to thank you.*

Shit, that reminds me I still owe him a Christmas present. I'm a terrible friend.

Or whatever I am to Drew.

I pull up my phone and go to our text chain.

The last thing that was sent was a message from him, an article from Psychology Today accompanied by the "mind blown emoji". I reacted to it with the exclamation points.

Because I couldn't think of anything else.

I type out my message and hit send. I've got about

twenty minutes before my next client and I need to take lunch. I grab the salad I packed from the minifridge and go to sit in my office.

My phone starts ringing before I can even sit down.

And I know exactly who it is.

"Hey, what's up?" I answer as if I haven't just texted him.

"You don't have to thank me, Dana."

My heart cracks. "Of course, I do, Drew."

"Seriously, it's not–"

"Drew, I've been a crappy friend, let me figure out something I can do in return."

Drew goes silent for a second.

Maybe I was a little too harsh. "Sorry if that was curt. I haven't been feeling myself lately and–"

"Look, I'm sorry. It's been a bit much, hasn't it?"

I collapse into my office chair and sigh. "Yes, but that's a me problem, not a you problem."

"I don't want you to feel pressured to get me anything or do anything for me or–" Drew sighs. "I'll stop."

I don't want him to stop. That's the whole thing. What girl wouldn't want flowers every week? I just don't want them from my best friend. I want them from something more.

"I just want you back in my life, Dana. And if you're not ready, I get it, but–"

"I am ready, Drew. I miss you."

"I miss you too."

I lean back and pound my fist to my head. *Fuuuuck.* "The whole Willow thing–"

"Wasn't fair to you."

"Made things *complicated.*"

Drew hesitates and then says, "Because we slept together."

"No, not that. Well, not *just* that." I look at the clock. Ticking down minute by minute until my next client is supposed to arrive. *Say it, Dana.* "Okay, I'm just going to—" I huff in frustration. "Don't you feel like we've been like...circling—"

"Thank god you said it, because I was way too scared to say anything." Drew stops. "Wait. Circling what?"

I laugh. "Like...something more. Than friends."

"Yes! Oh, thank god. That's what I thought you were going to say. I wouldn't have wanted to assume, but—"

"You're talking too fast, Drew. Slow down."

"Sorry, sorry."

I can hear his breath through the phone. Nervous. But steady.

"Let me take you on a date."

I feel every word I've ever known leave my brain.

"Or, sorry, that's a little fast, isn't it?"

No. Yes. But no.

"Your birthday is coming up. What are your plans?"

"I'm, um, nothing yet." It's still a week and a half out. Last year we had a big bash for my thirtieth and this year, I wanted something quiet, which to me will mean just a dinner in with my sisters and dad.

"Okay, then I'll take you out for your birthday."

"Drew..."

"Unless you don't want me to and you were bringing up the circling thing just to say that we should stop circling, in which case, well, I'll have to go bury my head in the sand out of embarrassment, but—"

"Drew!"

"Sorry, sorry."

I close my eyes. Imagine him as if he were in the room with me. Drew is usually a pretty smooth, laidback guy. But the moments he gets flustered are divinely adorable. Flushed faced, tongue almost visibly tied. I wish I could reach out and touch him. Comfort him. "You can take me out for my birthday."

A heavy sigh. "Thank god."

"No gifts, though. I still owe you your Christmas present."

"No gifts, yes. Promise, promise."

That is an empty promise if I ever heard one.

"The flowers really are beautiful," I say. "And I'm sorry you've felt the need to send them to me because I've been–"

"No apologies necessary. Maldives was what it was. I owe you millions of flowers for it."

I resist telling him that despite all the drama and the lying that so many moments of our time on the Indian Ocean replay in my head on the daily. I reminisce about those stolen touches and little looks, the ones we said were for show, but still made me feel like I was flying.

"I'll take care of everything. You won't have to lift a finger. What day of the week is that?"

"It's a T–"

"Tuesday, it's a Tuesday."

I smile to myself.

"Okay, then I'll pick you up right from work."

I flush. So many reasons to tell him "no". Just as many reasons to say "yes". Maybe more.

"I'll see you then. February second. Groundhog Day! You think he'll see his shadow?"

It won't matter. Because whether he sees it or not, Spring is going to come early for me.

14

DREW

I didn't bring flowers this time and now I'm regretting it. I waffled back and forth the entire time I was getting things ready for Dana's birthday this morning. I thought maybe it would be too much, but now, looking at the picnic blanket with nothing but a basket of food on it, I'm thinking I've done too little. I didn't even make the picnic food.

However, I scouted out a perfect location, picked out a perfect bottle of champagne, and, despite Dana's wishes, I brought her a gift. A small thing. Nothing flashy.

I got her sisters roped in to have it all set up for us once we got to the beach. That way I could still pick her up from work and have things ready to go. They must have skittered off the second they saw my car pulling into the lot.

"I know it doesn't look like much," I say, tugging on the sleeve of my flannel.

Dana laughs. "Please, Drew, don't be ridiculous." She throws her hand toward the ocean. Placid and smoky on the horizon. "It's perfect."

A picnic in February in LA requires a little bit of

bundling up, at least compared to our lifestyle the rest of the year. I've got my flannel, Dana is wearing a chunky sweater pulled over a slinky dress with a pair of perfectly white tennis shoes, which she has in her hand rather than on her feet.

"Should we sit?" I ask.

"Yes, I think we should."

We settle onto the blanket. My heart is pounding. I haven't seen her in nearly a month. The longest I've gone without Dana in my life the entire time I've known her, even when she was my grief counselor.

I've missed her. So much.

I pour us both a glass of champagne, the bottoms of which are laced with raspberries. "To you. Happy birthday," I toast.

"Thank you," she says with a shy smile.

Our glasses clink. I resist downing my champagne in one whole gulp. I'm so nervous. But Dana doesn't respect liquid courage. I'll take it slow.

"Um, I know this is a weird way to start a birthday celebration for *me*, but I actually have something for you," Dana says. She pulls a tiny box from her purse.

"*Dana...*"

"I owed you a Christmas present!" she says. "Take it."

I accept the box and shake it slightly. A little clattering inside.

"Careful," she warns.

I raise an eyebrow. "What'd you get me? Glass pennies?"

"Haha. Ass."

I grin. Been way too long since I've heard her tease me. I untie the twine around the box and lift off the lid. Inside is a tiny sailor figurine with a matching dog figurine, both kicking out their legs. "Are these–"

"Sailor Jack and Mac!" Dana exclaims. "From the Crackerjack box."

"Where did you find these?" I ask, lifting the little figures up and examining them. They're not very detailed, but it's only because they're *so* old.

"Etsy," she smiles. "You like them?"

"Like? Love, you know how much I love Crackerjack," I say.

Dana laughs. "You're the only person I know who still buys Crackerjack at the ballpark."

"I love these. They'll go on my desk at the office." Though my workplace is a little unconventional, it still has all the things an office is supposed to have. My entire top shelf is manuals mixed with meaningful trinkets. "They'll look great next to my Dodgers Pez dispenser."

When Dana is extremely happy, her shoulders tighten, her chest swells, and she clasps her hands together at her waist. Not to mention the smile on her face, so big, but resisting being toothy. "When I saw them, I knew you had to have them."

I want to lean over and kiss her, that's how much I like the gift. No, actually, that's just how much I like her. "Well, since we're starting with gifts..."

"Oh, stop that–" Dana flips open the top of the picnic basket. "Let's eat first."

***

I THINK about the gift at the bottom of the basket the entire time we're eating. I keep trying to give it to her, but she stops me at every turn.

"Not until I'm *full*."

And boy, can this girl eat. She's always had the appetite of a competitive eater, but even this is impressive. It's like she's forcing me to wait, be patient.

However, if the last month has taught me anything, I would wait a long time for Dana. A lifetime even.

She polishes off a chocolate covered strawberry, the red juice dripping over her lips, making them even redder than before.

She's making this so difficult.

"Mm-mm-mm..." Dana says, smiling. "That was amazing."

"I made it myself."

She slaps my arm with the back of her hand. "Liar. You can barely boil water."

I laugh. I grab the delicate, long box out of the basket. "Present time."

She rolls her eyes. "I told you not to–"

"You have to *know* at this point I'm always going to bring a gift," I say, rolling my eyes.

Dana blushes. "I know. You're so thoughtful."

My heart flutters. "Okay, here. Open."

Dana takes the box, unwraps it messily. That's one thing I love about her. She's so put together, so mature, has her eyes on everything. And then these funny little habits like being unable to unwrap something, even an envelope, without tearing it apart.

I've got it bad for her. Really, really bad.

"This better not be jewelry," she says, eyeing me when she realizes it is, indeed, a black bracelet box.

I smile bigger. "Open."

Dana's forehead tenses and, for the first time since she's arrived, my heart drops into my stomach. Maybe this wasn't a good idea.

However, all those fears disappear when she opens the box and her face alights. "Oh, my god."

"It's a—"

"Did you make this yourself?"

I nod.

"Stop it! Drew!" She pulls out the braided bracelet, strands of all sorts of brightly colored thread making an intricate pattern. "You *made* this?"

"Yes."

"I didn't know you made friendship bracelets."

I had thought about making her something a little fancier. I do metal work, I could have made her a cuff with some gem stones or something else, but I thought that might have been too much given how tenuous everything is. This seemed like a good first step. "Well, you know, growing up with only a mom, I did a lot of things boys don't normally do. At least when we were kids."

Dana smiles. "Put it on me, will you?"

She holds her wrist out to me. Delicate, beautiful. Would love to kiss it. Would love to kiss every part of her body. Worship her. Keep her. Make her mine.

Only if that's what she wants too.

And today, I'm determined to find out if these two years of friendship have set the stage for something much more. Much bigger.

I take the bracelet and wrap it around her wrist carefully. "This isn't just a gift. It's sort of a symbol."

I'm not good with the mushy words. Something Willow didn't like about me. The reason when things have started getting serious with most anyone, I've run the other way.

Not anymore.

"It's to let you know that no matter what, I'm always

your friend. First and foremost. If we grow into more, then I will welcome that...you have no idea how I would welcome that."

Dana giggles. Good sign.

I tie the ends of the bracelet in a knot. "I will always be here for you. You're my best friend. And without you the past month, I literally felt like I lost a piece of myself."

She starts to open her mouth.

"I know you're going to give me your whole counselor spiel and say that 'You can't attach to people and not be open to the possibility of losing them', or whatever, but–"

"You know me too well."

I meet her gaze. Her warm brown eyes pull me in, cutting through the cool beach breeze. "Yes. That's the point. I know you so well. Better than I know myself."

Her lips part. Perfect to kiss.

That's not a line I can cross yet.

I swallow. "I want to be with you. I've wanted it for a long time, Dana."

"How long?"

"You really want to know?"

"Yes."

"Two years."

"Drew..."

I hesitate. "Actually, technically, longer than that. Because I actually stopped our sessions because I had feelings for you, so...Two years and change, really."

Dana is quiet. Her chest rises and falls with a nervous breath. I hope I haven't ruined everything.

"Too tight?" I ask about the bracelet.

She shakes her head, curls wavering. "No. Perfect."

I start to draw away, but she grabs my hand, pulls herself toward me and kisses my cheek softly.

"Thank you." Her whisper causes goosebumps to break out all over my body. "You have no idea what you mean to me."

"Dana—" I touch her cheek and pull away so we can look at each other. "You have no idea what you mean to *me*."

Her eyes are full of love, but her lips are screwed tight together.

"What is it?" I ask.

"God, Drew. I'm scared."

I chuckle. "Me too."

"I don't want to ruin this or hurt you or hurt *me*. Anyone."

"I recall someone—"

"Ugh! Don't use things I told you in counseling against me! It's annoying!"

We both laugh.

"You're a good teacher. A lot of it stuck. What can I say?" I say with a little shrug.

"I just don't know if it's fair. That I know so much about you. I've heard you express your deepest thoughts and fears to me in confidence."

I smile. "That's good! You know me so well—"

She shakes her head. "But, Drew. Some of those things scare me."

My smile falls.

"And that's not fair to you. For me to come into a romantic situation knowing all this about you and—"

"You don't know everything about me, Dana," I say abruptly.

Her eyebrows jump up.

"Like my dad. You don't know about that."

Dana nods slowly. "You don't talk about it, that's true."

I swallow.

"You don't have to. You don't have to reveal everything to me in order to be..." Dana shakes her head. "You know, with everything with my mom, I'm just scared of people leaving me."

Dana doesn't know how I've been left too. She knows about my absent father. But she doesn't know just the extent of how that impacted me. How he hurt me. I've never been able to tell her about it. And I'm not sure I can now that she's expressing her fear of being left. After everything with her mother, I can't imagine how hard it is to trust people. At least my dad had one foot out the door the whole time.

"I'm never going to leave you," I say.

"You don't know that," Dana immediately says. "People change. What they want changes, who they want changes, you can't—"

"Dana, do you trust me?"

Her face twists.

Maybe she doesn't.

"I don't trust anyone. Not even my own sisters sometimes."

I slide my hand back through her hair and lean my forehead against hers. She doesn't draw away. In fact, I feel her wanting to move closer. "Let me be the person you trust without a shadow of a doubt, D. Please. You have no idea what kind of honor that would be."

We breathe together for a few moments. And somehow, all that breath propels us into a kiss. One kiss. Long, chaste. Sealing shut what chaos was opened in Maldives. Not shoved away where no one can look at it.

Right here for the world to see.

Dana pushes her chest toward mine, our clasped hands

landing against her sternum. Another kiss. Longer this time. When her lips draw away, she whispers, "I don't want to hurt you."

"Someone once told me that we can't control what hurts other people, but we can control our intention behind every action."

She smiles. "Sounds like a wise person."

"I think it was Confucius or something."

"Shut up and kiss me."

"Yes, ma'am."

IT BECAME VERY clear very quickly that what we needed to express to each other should be behind closed doors, not on the beach. Hands drifting lower, warmth building in the pits of our bellies.

Not something that should be seen in the middle of the day on Venice Beach.

We considered returning to the car, but quickly agreed that car sex would not suit the moment. So, we waltzed over to one of the hotels on the beach, booked ourselves into a room, and hurried into the elevator. Once the doors closed, we were on each other, mouths pulsing with heat, hands gripping whatever we could get a handle on.

It felt amazing.

But it feels even more amazing to be with her in this hotel room with a view of the Pacific.

Dana breaks away from me to go look out the window. She's just as beautiful from the back as she is the front. I can't wait to get my hands on her.

"Music?" I ask.

She smiles over her shoulder at me. "That'd be good."

I find the Bluetooth sound system and connect my phone. Organ music starts pouring out of the speaker.

She laughs hard. "'Take Me Out To the Ball Game' might be the least sexy song in the history of the world."

I walk toward her slowly. "Really? Have you ever heard the alphabet song?"

Dana tilts her head back, a peaceful smile on her face. "I was thinking more of something like Marvin Gaye or–"

"Oh, sorry. Here." I pull my phone back out and look for 'Let's Get It On' on Spotify. The suspense is killing me, and I'm the one controlling it. The feeling of Dana gazing at me and knowing what's going to come next, though, is a feeling I'd like to live in for a long time.

She laughs, the slight tinkle of bells, and my heart expands. Her hips sway side to side as she continues to look out the window. To see the world through her eyes must be a very beautiful sight.

I toss my phone down on the bed and slink up behind her, winding my arms around her body and pressing my nose and mouth into her hair. Deep breath.

"What shampoo do you use?" I ask.

Another laugh. "Is that really what you're thinking about right now?"

"Foreplay," I reply.

Dana's head dips back onto my shoulder, her lips twisting toward mine. "We'll have to work on that."

I kiss her. Our lips click apart, that cinematic smooching sound. Perfection. I run my hands down her front, feeling the ridge of her ribs, then the softness of her belly, the juts of her hips.

Her breath hitches before her lips land on my jawline. My eyes flutter shut. How am I going to make love to her when every move she makes causes my mind to go blank?

Her hips continue to idle back and forth, back and forth, grinding against my crotch as Marvin Gaye croons through the speakers. Her lips turn into a smile against my face. "Should we finish what we started in Maldives?" she asks in a whisper.

"I'm not the only one who has been thinking about that, huh?"

"No, not at all...I would have probably had you right there if we hadn't been interrupted."

I gasp playfully. "You would not."

Dana shrugs, giggles.

"You're naughtier than you let on, D."

"You bring it out of me."

My eyes fall onto her lips. Bitten raspberry. I want to kiss her forever. *Forever* forever. I want to know every peak and valley of the crinkles of her lips, learn them as if it's a language. Because it is. I want to be the only person in the world to speak the language of Dana.

I clasp the fabric of her dress in my hands and kiss her again with the purpose of letting her know what to expect of me. Depth. Passion. Commitment.

I've been committed to Dana since the second I left our last session. I didn't know if I'd be able to keep her in my life, but by god, did I try my hardest. She became my best friend. And privately, I nursed the crush which eventually turned into...

I love her. I always will. But it's not time to tell her that. We've only just begun. And I need to keep things realistic. Maybe we'll pull back the curtains and despise each other.

However, I don't think that's going to happen, especially once Dana begins shoving down the waistband of my pants.

Without breaking our kiss, I stumble back toward the

bed. I sit on the edge, clumping her dress up around her waist and hurriedly trying to push her panties down. Dana clumsily does the same, but with her hands behind her back, it's harder to control her movements.

"Fuck, I'm hot," she huffs raggedly and tears her sweater up over her head, revealing the thin silk bodice of her dress. Her nipples are erect through the fabric. I can't help but lick my lips.

I slide my hands up to cup her breasts, massaging them tenderly as I press my hips up into her backside. "Dana..." I sigh into her shoulder.

She slides herself back and forth until my naked member settles into her delicate chasm. "You're big."

I hum in laughter. "Don't lie."

"I don't lie."

"You lie in a motherly way. Like in the way mothers think their children are beautiful."

Dana glares over her shoulder at me. "Fine. You're tiny."

I flush. "Okay, I take it back. Lie."

Dana grins. "I wasn't lying, I was–"

I take her by the waist, reposition myself under her, and sink the head of my cock inside. She gasps, her body tensing, then relaxing onto me. Dana straddles my lap wider, grabbing my knees for leverage, and sinks down onto me.

"God, I've wanted this so bad."

"Me too," I whisper.

I lean back on the bed and watch her as she bobs up and down on my cock, admiring the sheen of her as she coats me. Then the sounds she makes. Oh, the sounds. Divine. Small gasps and whimpers as she rides me. "You fill me so good, Drew."

I make a sound in return, but it's meaningless. How can

I think straight when her walls are tightening around me, constricting me toward euphoria?

Dana's getting tired, moving fast on top of me. I can't be a pillow princess forever. I wrap my arms around her waist and press my mouth against her bare shoulder. The exquisite line creasing against my mouth. Then, I being to jerk my hips over and over, no room for me to pull out, just jabbing myself at my deepest point, grunting eagerly into her neck.

"Oh, my god, Drew."

I growl, my name in her mouth the most perfect word she's ever said.

Dana grabs one of my hands, ripping it off her waist and placing it between her legs, right above where we meet. "Touch," she says raggedly.

The second my fingers lope across her sensitive bud, her walls tighten even further.

"Fuck," I curse. "I won't last."

Dana doesn't speak, but if she did, I'd imagine she'd say, "You don't need to." She aligns her fingers with mine and pushes them tighter against her clit, directing them in a circular motion. I get the message and begin to do it without her prompting. Her hand falls away and she sighs in deep pleasure, her voice creeping higher in pitch.

"You come first," I say in her ear.

"You come with me."

She turns to look at me and I capture her lips into a deep, hungry kiss, teeth knocking together, pinching at her lower lip. I've wanted her for years, but now I need her. Need her every second for the rest of my life if I can help it.

One thing at a time. Maybe make her come first, Drew.

My mouth traps Dana's cries of impending pleasure until I strike her just the right way and she rips her head back, howling in pleasure. Her pussy clenches around me, inviting me to come too. And I do, spilling deep inside her, thanking god for the precious invention of birth control so that I can be as close to Dana as possible. In this way.

Dana loops her arms back around my neck, nestling a kiss to my chin. "I feel you."

Those three words strike a part of me I didn't know was waiting to be awakened. To be felt and seen by Dana, the person I care for most in the world–

Yes. That's a fact. She's the person I care for the most in the entire fucking world.

I hope I can make her feel that. Not just with my words. But in the way my hands and lips find the most intimate purchases of her body. The way I look at her.

I feel you too.

Dana kisses me softly. One singular kiss without the eagerness of sex behind it. "We should do that again."

I grin. "Give me at least ten minutes."

"I'll give you twenty."

"Generous."

Dana's face lingers before mine, her nose brushing up against mine.

"What?"

She shakes her head. "Nothing. Just you."

If I didn't know better than to get my hopes up, I'd say there are things Dana wants to say just as badly as I do, things that may have been creeping onto her lips for two whole years. Things that would be ridiculous to say so soon after we've decided to take this first jump together.

No. I won't get my hopes up that Dana might love me just as I love her.

I have to earn that.

Besides, words don't compare to the way I feel softening inside her. No rush to leave. Nowhere to go.

All we have to do is be here and now.

15

———

DANA

IT COMES AS A SURPRISE TO NO ONE THAT DREW AND I are now officially dating. There was no use keeping the secret since my entire family has been encouraging it for nearly the whole two years we've been friends.

"About time!" Kira announced and went to pick out a very expensive bottle of champagne after I had managed to corral all my sisters and dad into the family home for our monthly breakfast.

It's hard to take things slow. I mean, two years is slow enough. We've gotten to know each other so intensely through that time that our relationship just seems to easily transition into romance. The only added thing is the sex and that is a major benefit.

Okay, not the only added thing.

It's all the little things too.

The touches, the kisses, the way we can openly look at each other lovingly and not be afraid the other might catch us.

So, after two weeks of our newfound relationship, it only makes sense that we're looped into date night.

And since it's our first date night with my sisters and their partners, Hunter has gone all out, clearing out the entire restaurant at his luxury Malibu resort so that we can have an incredible view of Point Dume while we drink entirely too expensive cognac and eat canapés topped with caviar that make Drew gag.

"I feel a little bad we're all here without Kira," I say, chewing on my lower lip.

"Oh, don't feel bad. I invited her," Amy replies. "She sends her regards."

"That's a kind way of putting it," Harley says with a sneaking smile. "I recall the exact quote as, 'I hate being the third wheel let alone the ninth. Hard pass'."

Gillian tosses her hair out of her eyes and leans back in her chair, looking at Axel beside her. "I'd say I could set her up with one of Axel's friends, but—"

"All my friends are already taken," Axel says with a knowing look to the table.

I smile to myself; this is what I've been craving. Intertwining my life with those of Amy, Gillian, and Harley. I felt peripheral until now. All of them growing up and starting their own families, bandying together like it's a little club. I know I had to earn a membership. And I know they hadn't meant to exclude me. But man, does it feel good to have a membership.

"What's that smile?"

I snap out of my haze and look at Drew. He's leaned over toward my ear, a curious smile on his lips.

"What's *that* smile?" I ask in response.

He leans in and kisses the lobe of my ear. "Asked you first."

"Oh, my gosh, you two are so sweet it's sickening!" Amy claps her hands together, clearly not sick at all.

I blush.

"I bet you're kicking yourself over how long it took to get here, huh?" Grant asks in his low, warm voice. Harley elbows him, but they share a tender look.

"I have no regrets over how long it took," Drew says clearly and takes my hand under the table. "Otherwise, it wouldn't feel as good as it does."

Gillian wipes fake tears away from her eyes. "I'm going to cry."

"Enough about us," I say. It's a little overwhelming to be the center of attention. I haven't been the center of attention since I was the only Solace girl. That was barely a whole year of my life before Gillian came on the scene. Then, as I got older, all I did was shove my sisters into the spotlight, celebrating them, supporting them, making sure the spotlight stayed off me.

I'm not sure I'll ever be able to handle it. Luckily, though, having Drew at my side makes it way easier.

"She's blushing. Quick, change the subject," Harley says teasingly.

I glare at my little sister and she simply beams in response to me. God love them all.

"Well, we have a tentative launching date for the Seton Lot. We are aiming for a grand opening for the playground early next year," Axel says with a pleased smile.

"Wow, that's great!" Drew says, leaning onto the table.

Axel chuckles. "Yeah. We figure it should be around March, so that we take the time to make sure all is safe and built as sturdy as can be. We want it to be the best park there is and we are working hard for it. It might be a bit longer than we wished for, but slow and steady wins the race, right?"

The corner of Drew's lip perks up. I want to kiss that

corner, feel the scratch of his facial hair. But one kiss always leads to more with us. Another, another, another, then the clothes are off and then we're diving between each other's legs, wishing for more and–

"God, you're obsessed with him," Amy says, nudging my arm.

I blush again, even harder this time. Part of me wishes I could keep it together and not look like such a lovesick dummy. But I am a lovesick dummy. And the part of me that loves being one always seems to win out.

"...a big concert and outdoor picnic. Get the kids involved," Axel goes on, talking about whatever opening day plans he has for the playground. Gillian is listening with rapt attention although I'm sure they've discussed this ad nauseum. She's proud of him and I'm proud of her for that. They've come a long way since last summer. Not even together a year and I've seen a major change in both of them. Axel, certainly, going from single guy to father in the blink of an eye. But Gillian too. She's not gripping quite so tightly, not trying to control everything.

"Seton must love you for that," Hunter says.

"You bet they do. And I'm sure there'd be a place for Jessica if you wanted to admit her," Gillian responds with a broad grin.

Hunter shakes his head gently. He might look like the lax surfer type, but he's a hotel magnate through and through. "We're going to go private, but thank you for the offer."

Gillian could certainly afford to send Stella to a private school, especially now that she and Axel have matching wedding bands, but she's still the free spirit we know and love. "Suit yourself. More playground for us," she says with a shrug. "What about you two? Where is Tana going?"

"Tana's not even one!" Drew says with a gape.

"We're on a waiting list for Harcourt," Harley answers, ignoring Drew's interruption.

He looks at me with shocked eyes. I shake my head and shrug. "Private school is nuts," I say with a meek smile.

"It's for security purposes, of course," Grant says, clearing his throat. "She'll have to go private in order to assure that. Given my visibility." Grant's running of Infinium certainly makes things complicated when it comes to normalcy for their daughter.

"Plus, if we start sooner than later for Tana, then we'll have an open door for the next baby."

I choke on my cognac and not because it burns like a mother. "*Next*?!"

"Oh, my god. You're pregnant?!" Gillian gasps, grabbing Axel's arm.

Harley waves her hands through the air. "No, no, no, I'm not–"

"Next baby, Harley. *Next baby*," Amy says adamantly.

"I know what I said! Yeesh! You all are like hungry tigers when it comes to syntax and word choice, huh?"

I look to Grant for more of an answer. Harley can be edgy, especially when she thinks we are purposefully misunderstanding her.

He laughs slightly and then flushes. "We're not opposed to another child, that's what she means."

"We're *trying* is what I mean," Harley says, conceding.

I smile, although there's a slight pang in my heart. Harley and Grant are already starting on their second baby and I've had a boyfriend for two weeks. I have so much catching up to do and I don't know how I'm going to do it.

"I never understood why people tell other people they're trying for a baby," Amy says with a sniff of the air.

"You might as well just tell us you're all going to bang when you get home."

"Okay, we're going to bang when we get home," Harley says.

Amy spits out her drink, thankfully away from the table so none of us ends up in the splash zone.

"That's so gross, Harley," Gillian says with a roll of her eyes.

"That's what she told me to say!" Harley defends.

I roll my eyes and mutter to Drew, "They're unbelievable."

He grins. "They're hilarious."

I feel wrapped in the warmth of his arms even though his hand is simply on the back of my chair, tip of one of his fingers tracing a line against my skin, back and forth. Drew doesn't just know me. He knows my family. He knows how important these wonderful, ridiculous women are to me. And the men they love too.

"Besides, I have a feeling Harley and Grant have a lot more in common with you and me than you'd like to let on," Drew says and drops a kiss to my shoulder.

Heat radiates between my thighs. Yeah, he's right, I don't want my little sisters thinking about my sex life.

However, once *my* mind gets on the topic, it's hard to get off it.

In fact, we were late in getting here because when Drew came to pick me up, he pushed me back into the living room, right onto the couch, pulled my legs into the air and ate me out until I reached infinity.

Lord knows what we'll get up to later.

I certainly can imagine a few things, though.

"We have the next three already planned out, thank god," Amy announces.

I recoil back into reality, begrudgingly. Imagining Drew's body up against mine is a much more enticing task for my brain.

"A far cry from last summer," Amy says with a shake of her head.

"I forgot about that," Gillian says, shaking her head.

"I didn't," I reply. I was up with Amy late into the night when her insomnia was getting bad last summer. Between her editor being unsatisfied with all her book ideas and the complications of her relationship with Hunter growing heavier by the day, it was a dark time.

I'm certainly glad they're sitting side by side, an engagement ring on her finger, and a sigh of relief on her lips. That's what my littlest sister deserves.

"What are they gonna be about?" Drew says, nudging one of the canapés on his plate, trying not to wince at the little fish eggs clinging together.

Amy smiles up at Hunter. "Petunia's dad is getting remarried. So there's going to be a whole series about her meeting her stepmother and how they become friends and–"

"Something tells me this is autobiographical," Axel says with a smirk.

"Well, yes, parts of it," Hunter answers, leaning back in his chair and crossing his leg. "Except Amy won't be Jessica's stepmother. Once we're married, we're going to get adoption papers drafted and..." He trails off as he looks at Amy.

Drew leans over to my ear. "I think he just got lost in her eyes."

"I think you're right," I reply with a giggle.

I feel Drew staring at me, so I finally draw my gaze to

him. And just like Hunter, I find myself getting lost too in the field of periwinkles in his irises.

"This doesn't feel real," Drew whispers.

The rest of the table has started celebrating Amy's eventual adoption of Jessica, leaving us to be in our own little world if only for a moment. "In a good way or a bad way?"

"*Good*, of course, good," he replies. "Like I'm in a dream. A really good dream."

I kiss his nose. "Feels pretty real to me."

Drew ducks his head away, reddening around the nose.

What a bashful, dopey dummy. All mine.

Secretly, I can't wait until it's our turn to sit at this table on date night and divulge our own news. Vacations, moving in together, an engagement, wedding...I'm getting ahead of myself.

This moment, with Drew accompanying me to date night, not as my friend, but as my date, is all I need right now. If it really is a dream, don't pinch me. I don't want to wake up.

16

———

DREW

I CLICK MY PEN SO FAST IT'S BECOMING WHITE NOISE. The engine blueprint hangs on the pinboard in front of me, marked up with red pen.

Click, click, click.

"What else? What else, what else, what else?" I mutter to myself, pacing back and forth.

It has to be perfect before I pull it up off the paper.

I focus in on a corner of the diagram and pull the pen up, hovering it over the drawing.

My phone starts buzzing over and over in my pocket. A call.

When I check the screen, the whole world drifts into the background and a smile spreads across my face. *Dana.* I shouldn't be taking personal calls when I'm working, but I'll never deny her or myself an opportunity to talk.

Even if I just saw her this morning in my bed.

"Hey, babe, how's it going?" I answer.

Dana answers with a giggle. "Still not used to that."

I smile and pop into my desk chair, kicking my feet up on the desk. "What? *Babe?*"

"Yes. And I hope I never do. I like the way it makes me feel."

I hum and drop the pen on the table. Lean back, close my eyes. "How does it make you feel?"

"Your tone, Drew."

"What about my tone?"

"Suggestive."

I smile. "Sorry. Just love hearing your voice."

"We have to stop with this whole 'the feeling is mutual' thing."

"Do we? I think that makes for a very healthy relationship."

Dana sighs. "Not used to that either."

Relationship. Big word, especially for something so new. But there was no use wasting time on dating and being cautious. We've been preparing for our relationship for a long time. It's only felt more and more right with each passing day.

We've taken to spending nearly every night together, except for when she's visiting her dad. Her place, my place, alternating every night. I even have a toothbrush on her sink.

This morning, we awoke in my bed. She doesn't have clients today, so I let her lay there, peppering kisses across her back. When I went to say goodbye, she pulled me into bed by the collar, kissed me fiercely, and whispered, "Come home soon."

Home. We don't share a home together. And yet, we do. Dana is my home. Not my apartment. Not a place. A person.

I think she's been that for a really long time, actually.

If only my mom could see me now. See how happy I am.

"Anyway, Gillian invited us over for dinner tonight. You in?"

I sigh. "Yeah, I'm in."

"You're not."

"What?"

"You sighed."

"No, I'm happy to. I just—"

"I don't really want to go either, so if I can use you as an excuse..."

I gape. "*Hey!*"

Dana laughs. "What? Tell me I'm wrong."

Don't get me wrong, I love Dana's family. But there's been a lot of family time ever since we started dating. Any sane man would be overwhelmed beyond belief. Family dinners, date nights, ballet recitals, book launches, all the things I would normally have the ability to opt out of from time to time. Now I'm part of the clan which means...no backing out. "It's your call."

"Diplomatic as always."

I chuckle.

"I was thinking instead of dinner at Gillian's..."

"Yes...?"

"Pizza. Trash TV."

I clutch my heart. "God, you're a vixen. How did I get so lucky?"

"Not lucky. Just have a hankering for pizza."

"Detroit style?"

"Obviously."

The way we talk, so quick and clipped, is like a different language. I didn't recognize it before we were dating. Now, though, it feels like we're always working through a code meant only for us. "Dessert?" I ask.

She laughs, low and slow like a ristretto shot of coffee. "Is that even a question?"

I can practically taste the sizzling tang of her on the tip of my tongue. Tucking my tongue into her tight entrance, lapping her up for as long as she'll let me, wrapping my lips around her swollen clit. There's no dessert better than Dana.

"Ice cream sandwiches, duh."

I balk, my fantasy tainted.

I can hear her sneaking smile on her lips. "What else would it be?"

"You're a demon."

"You love it."

I love a lot of things about Dana. So many things I may as well say I love her. But not yet. Too soon still.

"What time will you be home?"

"My home or your home?"

"Mm, I'm still in your bed. Let's say yours."

I bounce my head against the headrest of the chair over and over. Still in my bed. Bet she smells fucking divine. "You'll need a drawer at this rate."

"That assumes I wear clothes around your house."

She's going to kill me. I swear. "Dana, I'm at work."

"Sorry, am I distracting you?"

The phone buzzes. I pull it back. Picture from Dana. A delicately arranged selfie of her body curled up under my sheets, her bosom only halfway covered, red nipples peeking out. I shake it off and put the phone back up to my ear. "You're going to get yourself hung up on if you–"

"Don't like it?"

Like? No. Love. "You're impossible."

"Hurry back, alright?"

Before I can reply, Dana hangs up. I take several

measured breaths and drop my phone into my lap. "Don't get hard, don't get hard..."

I would never deny her teasing. It's too much fun. I don't mind being half-hard at work. But I have to be able to focus again. I run my hands over my face and slap my cheeks. "Okay, Drew, get it together. Red pen, where's my–"

The phone buzzes again.

"Shit, Dana!" It might be driving me nuts but I'm not going to say no to another tease of what awaits me when I get home.

Except there's not another text from Dana. It's from a number not assigned to a contact. But a number I know.

Willow.

I feel like I might throw up.

> Are you seriously just going to ignore me?

Followed by a picture of her in a lacy set of panties.

I throw the phone away, my heart pounding.

Her text is the most recent in a string of unanswered text messages. I haven't deleted them in case the police need a paper trail to blame someone for my death. I'm quite close to defining the way Willow is trying to get my attention as stalking.

It hasn't just been text messages. Not by far.

It started back in Maldives. I was too wrapped up in Dana to take it seriously. She was...leaving me notes. Under the door of our hotel room. I managed to intercept all of them. Even though things had been strained between Dana and me, I wouldn't have put it past her to give Willow a piece of her mind. When it comes to the people she cares about, Dana doesn't back away from a threat.

They've been harmless.

Mostly.

Except for the few times she's sent me unsolicited pictures. I delete those right away. Obviously.

There have also been emails. A couple letters in the mail. A visit to the office that was a "just in the neighborhood" kind of thing, except Willow has never had any business being in Pasadena.

Okay. Maybe we do have a problem.

I stare at the phone on the ground and start to worry the skin on my thumb between my teeth.

I can't have Willow threaten my relationship. It might have started fake, but now it's real. More real than anything has ever felt. More real than things with Willow ever felt by far.

Swiping the phone up off the floor, I start to type out a message, ignoring the racy picture.

We need to talk. ASAP.

I need to stop this. Now. Before it gets worse.

Willow responds in seconds.

Yes, sir ;)

I just hope there's still time for me to fix this.

WE MEET at a Starbucks by my work. Nothing personal. Just a big box chain that means nothing to me or to her and definitely nothing to us.

"What do you want?" I ask when we get up to the counter, my jaw is so tight I'm afraid my teeth might break.

"You're buying? How sweet..." Willow says and strokes her hand down my arm. "Venti iced Americano, please."

The cashier looks at me.

I shake my head. "Nothing for me."

"I can't drink coffee alone, Drew," Willow chides.

I shake off her arm and reach into my pocket for my wallet. "Fine. Coffee."

"What size?"

"Small? Tall?"

"Whatever."

The cashier taps a few buttons on the computer. "Would you like room?"

"No, black. He takes it black," Willow interrupts and looks at me with insistence in her eyes.

God, she's starting to scare me.

This sit down can't come fast enough.

We grab out coffees and take a table by the window. "Well, I'm so happy you finally came to your senses and decided to reply to my text, Drew."

"I should have come to them a lot sooner," I say, folding my hands on the table.

"I agree. So, she's in the past, right? What's her name? Diana?"

I clear my throat. "*Dana.*"

"Right."

"No, she's not in the past. She's very much in my present."

Willow blinks wetly. "Well...I've never been much into ethical non-monogamy, but I guess–"

"No, Willow, you're misunderstanding. I'm seeing Dana. I'm not seeing you."

She frowns slightly.

"It's time you let it go, huh?"

"Let what go?"

"Me."

Willow shakes her head like she's just been electro-cuted. "I can't do that, Drew. That's ludicrous."

"What's ludicrous is all these texts. The emails. Those fucking notes."

"You sound mad."

"I *am* mad!" I growl and immediately regret it when I see how she flinches. "You've been trying to get under my skin for nearly three months now and it's time to stop, Willow. We haven't been together for five years. *Five years!* I've moved on. It's time you do too."

Willow recoils slightly, her eyes flicking back and forth across the table. "You led me on."

"What?"

"You...you said I should wait."

I shake my head. What the hell is she talking about? "I don't know what you're—"

"You *told* me I should wait. After your mom died, you said—"

"Oh god, Willow. That was so long ago. I said a lot of things."

She produces her phone and shows me a string of texts. From my number. "You *said* you'd come back."

I swallow and look at the phone. She's right. Right there on the screen is a text from me.

Wait for me. It might take me a lifetime but wait.

And in response.

I will.

Why the hell would I say something like that?

I know what Dana would say. "You were grieving," I can practically hear her whisper in my ear. "You couldn't stand the thought of losing anyone else. It wasn't right for you to say it, but I understand why you did."

Willow, though, doesn't understand. Her eyes are starting to bud with tears.

"Christ, Willow. I've moved on."

"I haven't," she spits viciously.

I nod. "I can see that."

"I waited."

We hadn't seen or spoken to one another since the breakup until we both showed up at Gillian's wedding. I find it hard to believe she was just sitting on this all these years.

Unless she really needs some help.

"Willow..." I say carefully. "I'm really sorry. But I've moved on and you should too."

Her lips thin. "You let me send all the notes."

"I never replied."

"Pictures."

"Willow—"

"You're a fucking asshole."

I sigh. "All I can say is sorry. So—" I grab my coffee and get to my feet. No use dragging this out any longer. "Sorry, Willow. I'm really sorry. You deserve—"

"Fuck you!" she cries out through clenched teeth.

I feel half the café's eyes turn on us. *Shit.* I know how this goes. They're all assuming I'm a total dirtbag. I need to get out of here.

"You led me on!"

I shake my head and start to walk away.

"You're a coward! Just like when your mom died!"

My blood runs cold. I keep walking.

"This isn't *over*, Drew. This—"

Her words are stifled by the café door closing behind me. Thank god. I rush to my car and drive off as fast as I can, half-expecting her to run after me and slam on the windows. As I drive, tears start to drip down my cheeks.

Fuck. Been a while since I've cried about Mom. Used to be every day, then every other day, then every week, then...

Grief is a motherfucker. I don't need her waving it in my face too.

I have regrets. Who doesn't?

I can't imagine going back to the office today. I drive right home. Before I go inside, I wipe my face clean and practice a smile in the mirror. Dana doesn't need to know about this. She doesn't deserve the stress. She has me. And doesn't need to question it for a second.

Dana is at the door before I even walk up the front steps. She's wrapped in my robe, her curled hair still mussed from my bed. Concern passes over her face. "What are you doing here? It's the middle of the day."

I don't say anything. Instead, I go to her, wrap her in my arms, and kiss her. Her hands clutch at my back with surprise before relaxing onto my shoulder blades.

"Mm. You okay?"

"Yeah, never better," I say, convincing myself. "Couldn't stop thinking about that picture you sent."

Only half a lie.

17

———

DANA

It takes like ten minutes to get down to Kira's office. The Wynters Corporation compound is a sprawling beachfront property that gives Google a run for its money. The whole way, I'm trying to calm my stomach. It's been in knots since I woke up this morning, alternating between uneasiness and nausea.

Definitely ready for a big lunch. Hopefully, I'm just hungry.

Kira is squirreled away in the basement like she's some secret that needs to be hidden from the light of day. What's the point of having a beachfront office if you don't even have windows?

When I get to her office, her door is open, so I waltz right in. She's hammering away on her computer like she's playing Beethoven, the clicking cutting through the air at a breakneck speed. I can see numbers flying across the reflection in her glasses, brown eyes zeroed in on the work she's doing.

I'm sure she notices me when I come in, so I go toward a seat along the wall.

"Don't sit. I'm almost done," she speaks out of nowhere, her fingers not daring to stop.

I catch myself on the arm of the chair and stand back up. "Alright..."

A few more seconds of typing, typing, typing, and then–

"Fucking hell."

"You good?"

Kira tears off her glasses and rubs her eyes. "Fine."

The bags under her eyes say otherwise. "How late did you work last night?"

Kira sighs heavily. "Does it matter?"

I laugh. "Yeah, it matters. Obviously."

"Yukon's launch has to be perfect."

"Is that the one that's–"

Kira nods, "Ethical expedited shipping."

That's not what I was going to say, but I'm glad she filled in the blanks for me. Kira is always working on some sort of app for Wynters. She's created so many from scratch at this point that I've lost track of all her accomplishments, just like I can't name every book in Amy's catalog. My sisters are incredibly prolific. "It's not going well?" I ask.

"It's going great *but* it needs to be perfect."

I shake my head. "Kira..."

"It does!"

"You always talk like your life is on the line. It's not."

Kira grunts gruffly in a way that indicates I couldn't possibly understand. "We've got a deadline. I'm working on all the bugs on our latest launch. When it comes to updates, we have mere hours before people say fuck all and move onto the next product."

"It's Wynters Corp. You're basically Apple."

Kira glares. "We're *not* Apple."

I gulp. "Duly noted."

After a moment, Kira's face softens. Just my little sister again instead of a terror desperate to squash out code bugs. I imagine they're cute and all pixelated with little pincers. Far from the reality she deals with. "Sorry. I'm just tired."

I cross my arms and smile. "You need lunch."

"Yeah. I guess."

There's a knock on the door behind us. Before I turn and look to see who it is, I clock Kira's expression hardening again. *Shit.*

"Am I interrupting?" A deep, male voice resounds.

I turn to find myself face to face with Kira's boss, Orlie Wynters. We haven't met, but I've heard enough about him to feel like I know him. Ever since he started the process of taking over for his father at the helm of Wynters Corp, Kira has been on absolute edge about him.

I smile. "Not at all!"

Orlie's eyes flick to Kira and then back to me, not a hint of pleasantry on his lips. The guy must know politeness, but whether he can give it with a smile is up for debate. "Kira, would you introduce us?"

"Y-yeah," Kira says. Her mouth is tight. "My sister, Dana. My boss, Orlie."

I'm tempted to give her crap for that introduction, but something in her eyes is telling me there's more to this story. "Nice to meet you. Heard a lot about you," I say, holding out my hand to Kira's boss. We shake. Big hand. Strong. "Good things, of course."

He shrugs his shoulders as if he doesn't care what has been said about him at all.

Wish I had that kind of self-confidence.

"What do you need?" Kira interrupts. It's almost as if

I'm not even in the room the way her eyes are locked on Orlie.

"Was just dropping in to see how you were doing on those bugs?"

"Great," she answers.

"Great," he retorts.

I look between the two of them. Two intense stares gazing back at each other. I can't tell if they're about to fight or...

Orlie breaks the tension, clearing his throat. "I didn't mean to interrupt. Kira's our best coder, you know, so I rely on her for our toughest jobs."

I smile at my sister, but her eyes have fallen to her desk.

"She's the brains of the family, that's for sure."

Orlie nods. "I'm not surprised." He checks his watch. I don't have to know the brand to know it's a small fortune. "Well, anyway, Kira, you should get some lunch."

"I will," she replies.

"Great."

"Great," she replies.

"Nice to meet you," Orlie says before striding out of the room with his head held high.

I respond in kind.

As I turn back to Kira, I start to say, "Well, that was weird..." but trail off when I see her expression.

She's got her chin propped up on her fists, eyes still glued to the doorframe as if Orlie still stands there. She sighs softly and the corners of her mouth creep up slightly. Eyes batting dreamily.

My god. Kira Solace has a crush. I've only seen in twice before. It's been years. Better not say anything else. If she knows people can tell, she'll shut down that part of her brain entirely as she is wont to do.

Time for a distraction.

"Lunch?" I ask.

Kira snaps out of her trance and jumps to her feet. "Please."

WE END up at a family-owned Greek place within walking distance of her office. We've passed several other cuisines on the way, but none of them sounded good. Settled for Greek because I didn't want to make her wait for a meal after working so hard.

However, Greek doesn't sound good to me either. I need something that will settle my stomach, not toss it like a boat on the ocean.

The second we walk in, I am hit with the stench of onions. It makes my whole body tense.

"Mm. Smells good. Can't wait for a gyro," Kira says, grabbing us a seat on the patio. Thank god. That way the sea breeze can carry away that intense smell.

I glance over the menu, looking for something that might settle my stomach. "What do you recommend?"

"They've got great spanakopita here," Kira exclaims. "They make it with dill and it's just delicious."

"Sounds good," I say, although not very enthusiastically.

"And the fish is always so fresh."

Fish doesn't sound very good either.

"But you can't go wrong with a gyro. They have a whole platter with meat and fries and pita. Onions and tomatoes. Mm."

"No onions," I say softly.

Kira frowns. "You off onions all of a sudden?"

"No, I just...seeing Drew later and–"

She snorts. "Have you ever heard of this new thing called a mint or a gum?"

I blush. "Just not interested in raw onions right now, alright?"

A server appears tableside, their apron covered in smears of food from the day. Clearly, they're not about appearances here, more so into the homegrown vibe which I would normally like, except the second he's in my atmosphere, the stench of onion returns.

My stomach flips.

"Hello, ladies, what can I get you? Something to drink to start?" he asks in a thick Greek accent.

I grab my napkin off my plate and stuff it up to my face. The nausea will pass if I just...

"Oh, Dana. You have to try the visinada," Kira says and then orders two for us.

I grip the side of the table. What the hell is going on?

"And can we get some saganaki to start?" Kira asks.

God, hurry up. I won't be able to hold it much longer.

"Certainly."

He starts to step away but Kira calls after him. "And between the Greek salad skewers and–"

I can't hold back a second longer. I launch myself up from the table and rush into the restaurant, uttering the word bathroom to the hostess and following the elegant line of her hand.

The second I slam into the bathroom, I'm bent over the toilet, retching every last bit of my early morning breakfast into the bowl and then some.

I've never had a particularly weak stomach. Never really turned my nose up at food in general.

And all of a sudden, I get a whiff of something aromatic, and I'm crumpled over the toilet bowl?

My mind goes one place and one place only. I'm not an idiot and I'm not going to kid myself. Sure, birth control is ninety-nine percent effective.

What about that other one percent of the time?

I need to talk to Drew. I can't do this on my own.

18

———

DREW

"Dana's in your office."

I blink at our office manager, Gina, who sits behind a big desk in the central meeting area like it's a war room. "Sorry?"

She peers up at me, raising one eyebrow. "You heard me."

The rest of my coworkers walk past me, filtering into their offices. We've just had a great meeting about my project. I have the go ahead to start making 3D printed mockups.

And now Dana is in my office. "Is everything okay?"

Gina shakes her head. "I don't get into your business, Drew."

I take a deep breath. "Thanks."

It can't be an emergency if it wasn't enough to pull me out of my meeting. Everything should be fine. Right?

I go to my office and find Dana sitting at the edge of my desk. When she sees me, her eyes go wide, almost like she's surprised I'm in my own office. And her face is beet red.

"Hey, is everything okay?" I ask.

Her fingers are curled around the desk edge, tense and white. "I..."

Dana doesn't finish her sentence. I stare at her, waiting for her to speak. Waiting for her to come to me. "What's wrong?" I ask as I cautiously approach her.

Her lips twist. I know that face. It's the face she makes when she's about to cry.

"Hey, baby, what's going on?" I touch her cheek softly.

Dana twists her face out of my hand. "God, I don't know how to say it."

I feel the world crashing down around me. My mind reels with a bunch of worst case scenarios, things she might say that will make my life shatter to pieces. She can't do it anymore. She met someone else. I'm not what she expected. Dana's about to break my heart.

I won't give her a reason to. I'll be strong. I have to be. "It's just me, D. Just me."

Her eyes tremor up to mine. "I think I might be pregnant."

That wasn't in my list. I'm not even sure I understood her correctly. Maybe this is a fever dream. "W-what?"

"I said I think I might be..." Dana's lips lift just enough to let me know that this is safe. This is okay. "I got sick when I was out with Kira for lunch and—"

"You weren't feeling well this morning," I say. The pieces are falling together. They fit.

"It's not a lot to go off of, but I just have this hunch."

I need to sit down. But I'm not going to let her see how weak I feel inside. "Did you take a test?"

"No. The second I realized, I came right here. Poor Kira is eating enough Greek food to feed a small family."

I gulp. Small family.

"Would you come with me? To the doctor? They were able to fit me in at four, and I just can't do this without you."

My chest expands. Dana needs me. Just as much as I need her.

"I know it's scary, but–"

"It's not," I say, my voice crinkling softly. "I mean, it is, but..."

Our eyes meet. I never saw myself as a father. Not for lack of wanting, but I never believed I would be fit for the role. However, Dana has changed everything.

She can change that feeling too.

"I know it's so fast. Too fast, but–" Dana starts to stutter.

"No, it's perfect. It's all going to be–hey, come here." I draw her into my arms and press my cheek against her temple. "I'm not going anywhere, Dana. Whatever happens."

Her arms slide around me, tight and unyielding. "You mean it?"

"Duh, D."

She laughs into my chest.

That's when it hits me. The potential for what might happen. Might *already be* happening. If Dana's suspicions are correct (and I've never doubted Dana, never for a second), then we're going to have a baby. Warmth pools into my belly. I might be holding both Dana and our baby in my arms right now. We might already be linked in the most intimate way two people can be. Right there inside her.

My heart starts to hiccup with anticipation. Dana always told me that anxiety and excitement are the same somatic experience. She never told me I might experience both at the same time.

One step at a time, Drew.

I kiss the side of Dana's head. "We'll be okay. No matter what."

———

I PACE BACK AND FORTH, trying to ignore the anatomical diagram of a pregnant woman on the wall.

"Drew, sit down," Dana admonishes.

"Sorry," I say and then sit back in my assigned chair. The second I'm down, my legs feel jittery again. I stretch them out and try to take square breaths.

"You'd think you're the one who might be pregnant, the way you're acting," Dana says with a soft smile.

I try to laugh, but it comes out more like a wheeze. "I'd almost rather it be that way. Then I wouldn't be responsible for putting you in a situation that–"

"Drew, you didn't put me in any sort of situation," she interrupts. "Seriously."

Her gaze is firm.

"You know I don't do well with doctors," I say with a sigh. Something I've expressed to her is how little I go to the doctor. After everything with my mom, I can't stand to be anywhere that's even vaguely hospital-y.

She smiles. "You're doing great."

Fuck. She's comforting me. What kind of man am I? We're about to get news that might change the course of our lives, will definitely affect her body more than mine, and I'm the one panicking? Jesus. Dana, though, doesn't look offended at my anxiety. All the fear that was apparent on her face the second I walked into my office has disappeared. "You seem...calm," I say.

"Is that a bad thing?"

"No, I'm jealous."

Dana tucks her hands under her thighs and shakes her hair out of her face. I hope our child has her blonde locks. Just as beautiful as her.

"Is it silly to say that having you here with me makes it feel less scary?"

Her saying that makes it feel less scary for me too. "Not at all."

Hard to believe only a month ago there was no us. Not like this. Now we're sitting and waiting for her doctor to return with results that will tell us if she's pregnant or not. It's amazing how quickly life can change. And for the better.

I watched my mom deteriorate from cancer before my eyes. That felt fast. Good things, I've believed, don't happen fast.

This good thing, though...seems to be happening faster than I can keep up with.

There's a knock at the door. I immediately spring out of my chair as Dana says, "Come in."

The doctor, I don't remember her name, smiles brightly and wafts in. I pace over to the corner. Like I'm in the way or something. *God, what do I do with my hands?*

"Well, I'm not going to keep you on edge. Your test results came back positive."

I run my hands through my hair. *Holy shit.*

"Really?" Dana asks. I can hear the hope in her voice.

"Yes. You're pregnant."

Dana looks back at me. Eyes glistening and mouth spread in a wide grin. "Did you hear that?"

I start nodding and am unable to stop. "Yep, yep. I heard that." *Get out of the corner and stop acting like a doofus.* I rush over to Dana's side and take her hand. Sparks fly through my body. Now it's official. She's carrying my baby. I can let that happiness flow through me unbridled. Especially given how big that smile is on her face.

The doctor laughs. "We'll get a better sense of how far along things are once your blood test comes back, but if you'd like, I can get an ultrasound tech in here to check out if we can pick up a heartbeat."

"Yes," I answer before Dana can. "I mean. Sorry, I–"

Dana smiles, leaning her head into my arm. "What he said."

"Okay, good!" The doctor smiles. "If there's one thing I like more than a happy mama-to-be, it's an eager daddy-to-be."

I swallow. Guess that's what someone's going to be calling me one day.

"I'll give you two a moment and send my tech your way," the doctor says and slips out the door.

Once it clicks shut, neither of us moves a muscle. Not for fear. Not for disappointment.

Have you ever felt so much joy you have no idea how best to express it? That no celebration feels quite right?

Dana, luckily, gets her wits first. She takes one of my hands and places it against her stomach, beaming up at me. "It's not much yet, but..."

I feel that warm feeling in my belly again. This time, I don't have to question it. Right there is a result of our desperate love for one another. Feels foolish that we haven't used the word aloud yet, especially when we now have a baby on the way. "No, Dana. It's everything," I say back.

Softly, she presses a kiss to my lips. "Are you happy?"

"Isn't it obvious?"

"I just want to hear you say it."

I slide my thumb back and forth across her belly. "So happy. Never felt so happy in all my life."

"Swear?"

"Swear on the Dodgers."

Dana gasps. "That's a big deal."

"Then you must know I mean it."

We embrace. Tight. I can feel tears building in my eyes, matching hers.

"I'm so happy too, Drew," Dana whispers.

We are bound together. In some way forever. "God, we move quick," I say.

"Some might say we've been moving too slow."

I tuck some hair behind her ears and then kiss her forehead. "Making up for lost time."

"Except we're doing everything backwards," Dana chuckles.

"Well, if you want, I could–"

"I'm kidding, Drew, I'm kidding. Please. No sudden movements. Finding out I'm pregnant is enough for one day."

I might have been half-joking. But where there's a half-joke, there's also a half-truth. Yes, it'd be crazy to talk about getting married after dating for only a month. However, we have two years of our friendship that this is built on. That's a long time of building. We took the leap. It only made sense everything tumbled quickly afterward.

Sure, marriage usually comes right after love. I'll settle for a baby. A baby with Dana is a dream I never knew I had.

Being the father of Dana's baby is the most important thing I'll ever do. I just know it.

The ultrasound tech comes in a bit later and has Dana put her feet up in the stirrups. Apparently, the ultrasounds you see in the movies don't happen until later in a pregnancy and Dana's doctor expects it's still quite early.

I hold Dana's hand, letting her grip in discomfort as the tech slides their device inside her.

"Okay, let's see if we can..." the tech goes quiet, focusing in on their screen.

Dana and I wait with bated breath. I bring her hand to my lips and kiss it.

Her blushing lips creep up again.

The silence of the room is interrupted by a rapid thrumming from the tech's machine.

The tech smiles. "There it is."

"There what is?" I ask.

"Heartbeat," Dana answers in a delicate voice.

I freeze.

"Strong too, especially given how early we're looking," the tech explains.

Everything else drifts away as I listen to the steady heartbeat of my child. I close my eyes, imagining what it will be like to feel that tiny beating heart once I have them in my arms. That's when the tears finally fall.

Dana wraps her arms around me, brings me to her chest. Holding me.

She believes in me.

I'm not my father. I could never walk away from this.

19

DANA

Drew and I have been on cloud nine for the past week. That's as long as we've been able to keep it quiet before I'm absolutely bursting at the seams to tell my family that I'm pregnant. I'm not like Harley or Gillian who can push all the secrets down into nothingness. I need someone to know. Everyone to know.

It might be a little early. First trimester is still so vulnerable and we have to be careful. But I'd rather have everyone know as early as possible to celebrate with us the whole time. And when I brought up telling everyone to Drew, he was incredibly encouraging.

"There's no reason to hide it. I don't want it to be a secret. Not at all," he said.

Which is why we're walking into family dinner at Dad's house wearing matching "Mom" and "Dad" T-shirts hidden under a sweater and a flannel (respectively). We'll wait for the right time to reveal and see if they can put the pieces together.

However, right when we arrive, I'm yanked into the kitchen by Gillian who is in desperate need to a sous chef. I give Drew a look of helplessness over my shoulder as I'm shoved away.

"God, it's *hot* in here," I exclaim the second the suffocating kitchen heat hits my skin.

"Dad doesn't have the air conditioning on," Gillian says. "Which I didn't know when I decided to make a whole quiche."

I look around the kitchen for any fragrant foods. Still sensitive to aromatics and I'd hate for everyone to start speculating because I hurled my guts out in the middle of dinner. I know Kira already has her suspicions.

All clear. Thank god.

"What can I do to help?"

"Oh, I don't really need your help, I just wanted to talk to you." Gillian pulls a stool out for me. "Sit."

I smile. I love being the sister everyone comes to. It's a lot of responsibility, but I'm secretly very proud to be the go to for all my sisters. The one they come to when they need a shoulder to cry on, an ear to lend, or someone to bounce ideas off of. I can imagine many women in my position would be resentful of that, having to pick up the slack for an absent mother.

Not me. It's my greatest joy. And I have to say, I think I'll make a great mom. Not just someday, but someday soon.

"What's going on, Gilly?" I ask.

She leans on the counter and heaves a sigh. She's clearly been rushing around for a while getting things ready for dinner. "Axel and I have been arguing about Stella's school ever since that night we all had dinner and–"

"Oh no..."

"He's feeling some weird FOMO that all his boys are sending their kids to private school. And I get it, I do. I don't want Stella to feel left out, but she's–"

"She's settled at Seton," I say, a bit of a mindread.

Gillian nods adamantly. "Exactly! She's been there for three years now. All her friends are there. And maybe the other parents aren't *billionaires*, but who cares? I'd rather her have a comprehensive understanding of the world and..."

Gillian continues to talk about the merits of Stella's schooling and the sniping arguments Axel and her have been having. I'm not worried, though. The two of them walked into their marriage knowing that they were both hardheaded as anyone. Somehow, it's what makes them work most of the time.

As she talks, I glance out the window and catch sight of Drew adjusting the collar of his flannel nervously. It was my idea to announce it in a silly way. He just went along with it because he's a good sport. Always has been. He's talking with my dad who has Tana balanced on his hip. She's freshly one year old. Can't believe how big she's gotten.

Drew leans in and tickles Tana's cheek.

Takes everything in me not to swoon. That's going to be us with our own faster than we know it.

"What do you think?"

I turn back to Gillian. Her back is to me as she opens the oven to check on the baking quiches. "Um...repeat the question?"

"Am I being crazy?"

That doesn't clarify anything, really. "Never, Gillian."

She straightens up and smiles at me. "Thank you."

Well, that was easy.

"Oh, my god, Dana. You're sweating," she says.

It is sweltering in this kitchen and, if I hadn't worn a shirt that has distinct messaging, I would have taken off my sweater the second I walked in.

"Come here, take this off."

"Wait, Gillian–"

Gillian comes over to me, undoes my cardigan buttons, and starts to wrench the sleeves down my arms.

"Stop! What are you–"

"Your face is red and–"

I try to wriggle away, but Gillian doesn't let up. The two of us might as well have been in the womb together, the way we paw at each other. "Gillian, stop it!" I bat her away and finally spin out of her grasp, scurrying over to the opposite wall to protect me.

"What is your problem? Do you want to die of heatstroke?"

I start to button my cardigan again, not caring if the buttons are mismatched with their holes. "Is there anything else you need to talk to me about or can I go outside and get some fresh air?"

Gillian appraises me carefully, eyes narrowed. "You're hiding something?"

"No, I'm–"

"Under that sweater. Let me see."

I stop in my tracks. "There's...nothing."

"You're such a bad liar, Dana. You've always been a bad liar."

"I pretended to date Drew for weeks in Maldives."

Gillian snorts. "Please, that wasn't pretending. That was preparing. You're with him now, aren't you?"

I swallow a big glob of something. Anxiety or nerves or...I don't know. My face is growing hotter by the second, not just because of the heat in the kitchen. And my eyes are starting to prick with tears of...ugh, I don't even know.

"Dana, what's going on?" Gillian asks, all of her attacking energy dropping to make way for tenderness.

I tip my head back to avoid crying. "God, I don't know why I'm crying."

"Seriously, Dana, you're scaring..."

Gillian trails off as I undo the cardigan and reveal the T-shirt. She stares at it with quirked eyebrows. "Mom?"

God, this was so stupid. We should have just announced it at dinner and then we wouldn't have to deal with this corny T-shirt thing at all.

"Where'd you get that?"

"Etsy."

"Why?"

I stare at my sister. "You don't get it?"

Her face starts to transform, eyes widening. "I might, but I don't want to assume something that's—"

"Your assumption is correct."

Her hands fly up to her mouth. "No."

"Yes."

I see her lips burst into a smile. "*No!*"

I smile back. "Yes!"

"Dana, you're—"

"Shh! Not so loud!"

Gillian keeps her hands pressed to her lips and starts jumping up and down excitedly, exclamations buried in her sealed mouth. She embraces me with all the thrust and intensity of her five-year-old self, and I laugh as she spins me in a circle with excitement.

"Who else knows?"

"Just you. And Drew, obviously."

"Oh, my god..." Her eyes twinkle with tears. "You're going to be a mom, Dana," she whispers.

Her uttering those words gives way to my tears. "I am."

And then we're both crying, sobbing excitedly. Gillian was the first of us all to be a mother. Years ago now, by accident (although nothing about Stella is an accident now). For once, the script is flipped. She's the one who can take care of me. And I already feel it in the way she's holding me, celebrating with me.

She's proud of me.

The door flies open. "How's dinner going?" Kira chirps and then stops in her tracks when she sees the scene. "What's going..."

Gillian steps away to show off my shirt. For Kira, it immediately clicks. "I knew it. I fricking *knew* it after you rushed out of–" She drops all her know-it-all energy and rushes to hug me too.

"What's going on in there?" I hear Dad's voice call out from the yard.

I straighten out my shirt and walk out into the yard, an apologetic look toward Drew. "Gillian made me."

Drew smiles lopsidedly. "Fine with me."

"What is this, *The Full Monty?*" Dad asks, not tracking what's going on.

However, Harley and Amy immediately clock my shirt.

"No!" Amy shouts.

"Yes!"

"*No!!*" Harley echoes.

My sisters all crowd around me, burbling congratulations and shedding tears.

"What is going on?!" Dad shouts out. He's never gotten a cute pregnancy announcement, so he's probably confused beyond belief. With Gillian, she was young and single and deeply worried about his reaction. Harley's pregnancy snuck up on all of us. This one might not have been planned, but for once, there's no reason to hide it from the light of day.

"Kent, look–" Grant grabs Dad around the shoulder and points at Drew's shirt. "*Dad.*"

Dad's brow is still creased in confusion.

Grant points at me. "*Mom.* Does that ring a bell?"

"I don't get it."

"And this man's a lawyer," Axel says, getting a snicker from Hunter.

I look to my sisters for that last boost of confidence I need to just come out with it. And their smiles are so wide. Wider than I've ever seen. "Daddy, I'm having a baby," I say, trying to smile through my tears.

Dad's brown eyes widen and his mouth goes slack.

"I'll take this, thank you," Grant mutters, swiping Tana out of Dad's arms. Tana laughs loudly.

"You're..." Dad shakes his head and points at Drew. "You..."

Drew and I gravitate toward one another, his arm sliding around my waist. "Yeah, we are."

We are. Drew and I *are.* We're an entity. One in the same. Hand in hand. Together. Creating.

Dad's hands go to his forehead. "I think I need to sit down."

"Daddy, stop it! You're being dramatic," Harley admonishes.

Everyone takes it very seriously; Hunter grabs Dad a chair and he falls right into it, eyes jerking back and forth to process.

I go kneel before him and take his hands. "Are you upset?"

"Upset? No, no. I'm..." He shakes his head and touches my cheek. "You're happy, Dana. All I've ever wanted is to see you happy."

My eyes fill with even more tears. "Daddy..."

He draws me up in his arms and holds me to his chest. I feel his heart beating.

"Are *you* happy?"

"Oh, Dana, of course I'm happy. I'm so proud of you. And you–" Dad reaches out a hand to Drew. "Come here."

Another hug, another tangle of limbs. Of love. The two most important men in my life, holding me with care and gentleness.

"I know you two are going to be great at this," Dad whispers.

Though I'm filled with an impossible amount of joy, I can feel the underbelly of it too. Like I'm waiting for the other shoe to drop. Everything is picture perfect. A boyfriend. A baby. A loving family.

I can't help but wonder when my streak of luck will run out.

20

DREW

"Thanks for coming up here to meet with me."

"Of course, Kent. I'm happy to." Happy isn't necessarily the word I'd use to describe it. I'm terrified to be sitting across from Kent Solace. I've never been terrified of the man before. He's always been affable and kind, inviting me into the fold of his family, even when I was just a friend.

Now, I'm much more than that. And that transition is something we have to negotiate.

After we announced the pregnancy to Dana's family, Kent pulled me aside and said he wanted to talk with me, "Man to man," which is a phrase I never thought I'd hear from his mouth given that he's a father for five girls and has always struck me as someone who doesn't lean into the "manliness" of things.

However, I wasn't about to say no to the grandfather of my child.

So here we are now, another day, another coffee shop. This one in Burbank, a quintessential haunt of Dana and mine and the whole Solace family.

"Coffee cake?" Kent asks, sliding a small dish of the pastry toward me.

They have the best coffee cake in the LA area, I'm convinced. Too bad I'm not hungry right now. Staring at Kent, not knowing what comes next, has left a lump in my stomach that feels like dense obsidian.

Again, though, I'm not about to say no to him. I take a dainty piece, thanking him, and gulp it down. I don't even taste it, that's how nervous I am.

Kent folds his hands on the table and screws his forehead together. "How's Dana doing with everything?"

"With...the pregnancy?" I ask. It's a word that still feels weird in my mouth, knowing that it's not a concept but a reality of my life.

Kent nods. "Yeah, you know, we're open with each other, but I'm still her dad. I know the girls all keep things from me because we don't have that bond of..." He hesitates. "You know, Gillian and Harley both had Dana to talk to during their pregnancies. Not that she had the physical experience, but she's always been the maternal figure in our family since—" He stops again. "You get what I'm saying?"

"Yes, of course."

"Dana doesn't have a Dana to talk to. Sure, they all support each other, but she's..." Kent takes a deep breath. "Life wasn't fair to any of us, but sometimes I worry it was most unfair to her. The eldest always gets too much responsibility and then to pile everything that happened onto that too, well..."

I smile. I don't want Kent to feel like he has to drag all the skeletons out of his closet. I know a lot about the pain of Aileen leaving them. He has no need to reopen the wounds for me to see.

"Dana is doing well. Nauseous. As to be expected.

Otherwise, though, it seems like everything is pretty standard for nearly three months along."

Kent smiles. "You sound like you know what you're talking about."

"Vaguely. As best I can."

"You're trying to be involved?"

I nod. "Yes, I think that's the least I can do."

"I agree." Kent takes a sip of his coffee. "I hope it doesn't feel like I've brought you here to your doom. I just...Dana's my first child. All my daughters have special spots in my heart, but the first is..." He stops. "You'll understand soon enough."

Kent isn't usually so serious. Dana has explained to me that she feels like he's always making up for the sadness they felt after Aileen left. Trying to be the fun, upbeat dad, always prepared with a quick joke or jab.

I don't know how to interact with a serious Kent.

"You'll take care of her, right?" Kent asks.

Our eyes lock. I've never noticed how similar his eyes are to Dana's. A light ring of green on the perimeter of brown. I can't help but think about my own child on the way. How will they take after me? After Dana? It's a crazy, swirling feeling. "Of course, Kent."

"She's special."

"I know that," I say and clutch my heart. "Believe me, I know."

His lips perk into a smile. "I know you know. I've always known you know that. After all, you've been following her around like a puppy dog for two years, so..."

I laugh. "You noticed too?"

"Of course I did! I might be oblivious to pregnancy announcements, but I'm not an imbecile."

I flush, laughing some more. I take another piece of coffee cake and nibble on it.

"I just don't want you to freak out since this is all moving too fast," Kent says, resetting the conversation to a serious space. "You know, Dana was an accident in her own way. Aileen and I weren't even married yet and we were still in college. And at the time, we were young and in love and it all seemed to make sense." He stops. "I've had to do a lot of thinking on that time in my life. If I made mistakes. Surely, I did, but having Dana was never one."

I remain quiet.

"I just want to know how serious you are about all of this. Because a baby is the most serious thing of all. And I'm no stranger to how backwards it all can be, but–"

"I'm a hundred percent serious about Dana."

Kent nods slowly.

"We haven't talked about marriage..." *Christ, we haven't even said we love each other yet.* "But that's obviously in the cards for me. As long as I have permission from you and your daughters."

Kent leans back in his chair, eyeing me carefully. There's a twinkle in his eye, the quintessential Kent Solace twinkle when he's being just a little silly. "Well, you have mine," he finally says.

"Thank you, sir."

"*Sir?* God, I didn't invite you here to be reminded of my own mortality, Drew."

"Mortality? You're still young yet. You're, what, a fresh forty?"

Kent blushes. "You're flattering me."

"Not flattery. If I didn't know you, I don't think I'd be able to guess you have five grown daughters."

"Again, the mortality thing, Drew..."

We both laugh and, as the dust settles, Kent relaxes in his chair. The confrontation part of the afternoon is over. "And how are you doing?"

"Me?"

"Yeah, the whole baby thing. Anxiety-inducing. I'm familiar. I did it five times, after all..."

"Surely it got better with each one."

Kent concedes with a roll of his eyes. "Yes, better. But it doesn't go away. Pregnancy is such a vulnerable time. And no one has really much control over the outcome. I was always jumpy when it came to Aileen's health and the babies. Not to mention the living creatures in my home. *Children...*"

I can't manage to laugh at that. My mind has been plunged into a dark pit of all the possible complications of pregnancy. Sure, Dana and I have talked some of them over. But in an effort to remain optimistic, I guess I've kept myself blind to the real horrors of what could go wrong in her changing body.

"I didn't mean to scare you," Kent says.

Shit, is it obvious on my face?

"I just want to know how you're doing with all of that."

"I..." God, how *am* I doing with all of it? It's been such a whirlwind since finding out we have a baby on the way that I'm not sure I've even stopped to consider myself.

Kent reaches out and touches my arm, squeezing supportively. "You can come talk to me about anything, you know? I care for you, Drew. And becoming a father can be isolating if you don't have a network of them."

I nod. "Thank you."

"I'm sure Hunter, Grant, and Axel would all have their own support to give you. But I want to be your number one.

After all, it's my grandchild," Kent says with a mischievous smile.

"Now you're the one bringing up the mortality," I say cheekily.

Kent throws back his head in laughter. "Suppose I am. And now *you're* deflecting."

I am. Because I don't know.

"You don't have to know."

Jesus, did I say that out loud? "I'm...overjoyed. Euphoric about the whole thing. You know how much I care for Dana. And if you don't–"

"I do. I can see it."

"Thank you. Yeah...yeah. There's no one else I'd want to do this with." I bite my lower lip.

"I am sure she feels the same."

"I hope so."

"I know so."

"Thank you. Again."

Kent sits and waits for me to reveal more. What is it about those fatherly eyes that just seems to bring all my emotions to the surface?

"I don't want to disappoint her. Or you. Or the baby."

"How would you be a disappointment, Drew?"

I shift uncomfortably in my seat. "I didn't exactly have the best role model when it comes to fathers."

"And you're afraid you'll end up the same way, huh?"

"Yes. Exactly."

Kent takes another sip of coffee and then grabs a big piece of coffee cake. "Just the fact that you're considering it and thinking about how you might impact the woman you love and your child already means you're going to be nothing like him."

I sigh. "You really think so?"

"Call it fatherly intuition. And don't worry, you don't have it yet, it will kick in. Sooner than you think."

"Yeah?"

Kent nods and, with a mouthful of coffee cake, says, "It's already happening to you. You just don't know it. But the carefulness you're feeling with Dana and wanting to make sure things are going alright, that's part of it." He swallows and looks off for a second. "The second it hits you, though, it's just going to be like a slap in the face. The best slap in the face, but still. A slap."

"When did you feel it with Dana?"

Kent does a double take; I wonder if I've asked something too personal until he starts to speak again. "Well, I guess it's when you start to be able to feel them moving. Mothers always get to feel that first, you know? But the first time you can actually feel your baby kicking..." Kent pauses. The rims of his eyes are red. "When that baby becomes really *real*. And you can truly conceptualize how much the woman you love is going through to give you another piece of her to love. It's–" He looks down into his lap.

I plan to have Dana forever. And Kent probably planned for the same with Aileen. It must be so painful to have beautiful memories tainted by who a person becomes.

Kent takes his napkin and wipes at the corners of his eyes, a smile bleeding onto his lips. "There's nothing like it, Drew."

21

DANA

"You should name your baby Stella. After me."

I smile at Stella as I stab my fork into my salad. She insisted on sitting next to me for our sisters-and-babies lunch outing and has been regaling me with a list of name options the entire time. "After you, huh? Wouldn't you be upset that you weren't the only Stella in the family?"

Stella frowns. Her green eyes roll up as she considers this. "Fair point. I'll think of some more names."

"Stella..." Gillian says warningly from across the table. "Baby names are very personal. If I had taken suggestions, your name probably would have been Prudence."

The little girl's face twists in disgust. "*Prudence?!*"

"I thought it was a nice name," Amy says with a shrug.

"Yeah. Sure you did," Gillian laughs. "No subtext at all with that one."

Amy ignores her and focuses on cutting Jessica's plateful of spaghetti for her.

"I can't believe I'm going to be the only one without a baby," Kira says with a shake of her head.

"I know. Who wouldn't want this?" Harley asks as she

pats Tana on the bottom over her shoulder. Tana has been alternately peaceful and completely inconsolable through our meal.

"Harley," Gillian chides.

Harley smiles and shrugs her shoulder. "You know I'm just kidding. But it's not all sunshine and rainbows."

"Except for me and Jessica," Stella says.

"Yeah, except for us."

"We're perfect."

"Mmhm. Sure you are," Gillian says.

Stella snickers. She's getting to that age where her sense of humor is really coming out, and apparently she can take a little teasing, just as much as she can dish it out.

"Is the food bland enough for you, Dana?"

I glare at Kira and she smiles to herself. I am not quite as good with the teasing as Stella is. Never have been, but now I can blame it on being pregnant. "Rude."

"Well?" Kira eggs me on.

"Yes. It's perfect." Never gone wrong with a Caesar salad.

"Announcement, announcement, announcement!" Jessica suddenly cries out in a sing-song voice I have to believe she learned in preschool. She looks up at Amy lovingly. The two of them might not be related by blood, but you'd never know it. I've been out with them on several occasions when Amy is legitimately complimented on how much Jessica looks like her. Amy blushes and takes the compliment and I know she loves it.

"That's one way to get our attention," Harley says, Tana now slobbering on her shoulder.

"Well, I have some news." Amy shakes her chestnut hair out of her face, her upturned nose making her look proud and elegant. "I'm officially moving in with Hunter and Jess."

"Shocking no one," Kira grumbles under her breath, loud enough for only me to hear. She might be working a lot of the time, but I know she's not eager to be our father's only roommate.

I make up for Kira's despondency with a big smile. "That's wonderful, Amy. When?"

"As soon as possible!" Jessica chirps. "That's what Daddy said."

Amy pushes some hair from her soon-to-be adopted daughter's face. "Well, I haven't told Grandpa yet...but yes, as soon as I can."

"Dad's going to cry, you know?" Gillian says carefully."

"Grandpa will cry?" Jessica reiterates, her lower lip pooching out.

"Grandpa always cries," Stella says dryly.

"*Stella*," Gillian admonishes.

I hang back as I usually do, waiting for things to get out of hand enough for me to step in. Mostly, though, I feel like I shouldn't get in the way. My dramas have always been quiet and internalized. And even though I've been the center of attention since announcing my pregnancy, I'll always be the eldest sister meant to keep the peace.

It's clear Amy is thrilled to be moving in with Hunter. They're engaged after all. "I'll be right next door. Dad will be fine," Amy says.

"Yeah, but now you've literally doomed me to living at home the rest of my life," Kira says.

"Doomed you? You love Dad."

Kira rolls her eyes. "Not the point."

"You can leave, Kiki," Harley says.

"I can't! Leaving Dad alone in that house? It's—"

"Sad," Stella finishes.

Gillian snaps at her little girl once more. "No one has children expecting them to stick around."

"Besides, maybe if you leave, that will start a new era for Dad," I say with a shrug.

"What kind of era?" Amy asks.

I look at Kira. "I mean...he should get out there. Find someone to—"

"Auntie Victoria..." Kira finishes my thought way, way ahead of schedule.

"Oh, no. Grant would hate that," Harley says, and then smiles devilishly. "We have to make it happen."

We spend the rest of our meal chatting about plans to get Dad and Victoria to realize how perfect they are for each other. At every major family event, when Victoria is in town, the two of them hover around each other the whole time like security blankets. Just like Drew and I have been the past two years. It's a match made in weird domestic heaven.

And we're determined to make it happen.

I DUCK out of lunch just a little early. I'm feeling exhausted, which I know I should expect given that I'm creating a whole human, but man, it's inconvenient.

As I walk to my car, I run my hand over my stomach. I'm starting to fill out ever so gently. Both Drew and I can tell. I place my fingers on the lower part of my belly where I first started to feel a firmness and smile to myself. It's becoming more real by the day.

My car is tucked behind a gigantic pickup truck which

is going to make backing out of the spot an absolute nightmare. Thank god for backup cameras.

When I round the truck bed, I'm surprised to find someone leaning against the trunk of my car.

And not just any someone.

"Hi, Dana."

Willow.

"What are you..." I trail off, keys dangling in my hand.

"Saw you and your sisters inside. Didn't want to interrupt but thought you and I could chat for a bit," she says with a smile that's feigning pleasantry.

I have a bad feeling about this. Even if she did see us inside, how did she know this was my car? "Oh, well. Hi, then. How are you?"

"Been better, honestly," she says, pushing herself up to standing and reaches into the back pocket of her jeans.

I take a half step away from her. Something is off.

Thankfully, she only pulls out her phone. "You should see this."

Willow sticks the phone right in my face, so close I can't read it at first. As my eyes focus, I realize I'm looking at a text chain. To Drew.

There's a picture of her in her underwear.

Then a message from Drew.

We need to talk. ASAP.

Followed by:

Yes, sir ;)

I frown. "What is this?"

"I'm just letting you know, he isn't who he says he is.

And I like you, Dana. I do. I don't think you deserve to be hurt."

I swallow and look at the texts again. Drew's "We need to talk" doesn't seem positive. But the way Willow is looking at me with sadness in her eyes doesn't help. "So, what happened after these texts?"

"We met up for coffee. Don't worry. He didn't cheat." Willow shrugs. "Not yet."

Willow is not a girls' girl. I know that much. In fact, I knew it when Gillian was just a kid and Willow was still a part of their friend group. She was the type who'd push you to tell you about a crush and then, once she knew, would go after him so you could never have him.

Not a girls' girl at all.

"Look, I'm not a perfect person. I've had my heart broken just like anybody else. But you'd think a guy would stay with the girl who supported him while his mother was dying."

I frown. "It's not that simple."

"Right, I forgot, you know all about that time in his life, being his counselor and all." She hums in laughter. "Isn't it funny I drove him right into your arms?"

"It wasn't like that at all."

Willow holds her hands up innocently. "I'm not claiming to know. Sorry."

We stare at each other.

"I just thought me and him were bound. After he chose me over her."

My brain is starting to spin. I'm exhausted and this isn't helping. "What are you talking about?"

"Oh, he didn't tell you? Drew was with me the night his mother died. Instead of with her."

I start to open my mouth to retort, but I have nothing to say.

I didn't know that.

"Us and a couple friends. But still." Willow shrugs. "He went home with me. And he wasn't with her when she died."

I knew that much. But Drew always said it happened while he was asleep. At home. I guess he was asleep. He just wasn't alone.

He chose to be with Willow instead.

There's more to this story. I'm not willing to take Willow's word for it, especially when she has me cornered in a parking lot.

"Just be careful. He seems all sweet and nice. But he's selfish. He does what he wants when he wants to. Doesn't stick around for too long. Especially when things get hard." She shrugs. "But what do I know?"

What does she know indeed. "Did you follow me here?" I ask.

Her face contorts angrily. "No, what the fuck? You think I'm a stalker?"

"You're texting my boyfriend and waiting by my car. That feels kind of in the realm of–'"

"You're not important enough to stalk, *Dana*," Willow spits.

I clench my jaw. There are a million things I want to say, but all of them will just escalate the situation to impossible degrees. I push past her and go to my door. "Well, thanks for letting me know."

"You'll do what you have to do, won't you?" she asks after me.

I dare to look back at her. And the sight makes me sad. Her face is full of hope. She wants to be with him so much.

Or the idea of him.

But I love him. Everything in her head is a story. I have the reality.

"Willow, you should know that Drew and I are going to be having a baby."

The hopefulness fades. Her mouth falls ajar. "What?"

I immediately regret telling her. If Willow is unhinged, who knows what she might do to me. To Drew. To our baby. "Hey, if you want to talk to someone about how you're feeling, I know some–"

Willow shakes her head and walks off quickly, disappearing through the labyrinth of cars.

I hurry into the car and lock the doors, my hands shaking as I put the key in the ignition. I shouldn't drive like this. *Deep breaths, Dana. Take a beat. Reset.*

So many questions are swirling in my head.

One: how did Willow find me?

Two: what were those texts really about?

And three: what will get her out of my fucking life?

Willow has faded into the background for me since Maldives. But clearly she hasn't for Drew. And while I find it truly hard to believe he's entertaining her text messages with any semblance of interest, I can't help but be cautious.

I'm having his baby, for god's sake.

I thought I could trust him. Fully. Without looking like a total schmuck.

Now, Willow has just thrown in my face that Drew has secrets he hasn't told me. I was foolish to believe I knew him better than anyone just because I've been his counselor. Everyone has secrets. No one can be trusted.

Not even my own mother.

So, how am I supposed to trust a man?

Answer: I shouldn't.

I run my hands over the steering wheel, back and forth, feeling the grooves against my palms. It's centering in a strange way.

I have me. I have my sisters.

And I have my baby.

Whatever happens, this baby is mine, truly and fully. And I'll make a beautiful life for them. They will be able to trust *me* without question. Always.

Believing that is the only way I'm going to be able to survive.

22

———

DREW

I thought I'd be bolder sitting next to Dana in a darkened theatre. But my nerves are abuzz. I feel locked in place. Afraid to upset the ecosystem of the darkened theatre.

I look askance to Dana, hoping she looks at me too.

She doesn't. She stares placidly forward, face aglow with movie magic.

Fuck. How do I get her attention?

I hold the bucket of popcorn over into Dana's lap and shake it.

"No, thanks."

"Oh, come on. I can't eat all of this by myself."

She gingerly bats the bucket away from her. "Not hungry, Drew."

I recoil and stick the blasted big bucket into my lap, chewing on the inside of my lip. Ever since I picked Dana up this evening, things have been off.

Hell, things have been off since a couple days ago when I called her and she didn't pick up, instead sending me a text that simply read,

"Not feeling well, talk tomorrow."

That sent me into a tailspin thinking about the baby and all the things that could possibly be wrong. What kind of pain was she feeling? Where was she feeling it? I sent a slew of follow-up questions.

The response I got was only two words.

Just tired :)

If it hadn't been for that smiley face, I would have felt like dying right there. For the past three days I've been living on that smiley face. But the second she got into my car and smiled at me in real life, I knew something was up. I know her too well for her to try and skirt around her problems like this.

Of course, I have no concept of what she's really going through. Her body. The changes.

But she's still Dana. She's still the person I care for most in the world.

"Thank you, though."

I look back at her. She's smiling at me. A sadness in it. Still, a smile.

"No problem," I reply.

Dana leans over and kisses me softly. It lingers the slightest bit. Given how I've come to learn her body, I get the feeling there's something way more behind this little kiss. A deeper want.

I kiss her back again, harder this time. The movie, a fucking romcom that we picked just because it was something to watch, fades into the background as my tongue sneaks under hers. Well, at least I have this. I know she wants me in some capacity. Maybe I'm overthinking it.

Maybe the pregnancy is really just bringing out some new emotions she doesn't know how to deal with yet.

I just wish she'd talk about them with me.

Dana wraps her hand around the back of my head, kissing me harder. My body lurches. The bucket of popcorn tumbles out of my lap and onto the floor, spilling everywhere. "Shit!" I curse softly. I start to lean down to clean it up, but Dana grabs me again, pulling me back to her. She leans herself over the arm rest between us, practically crawling into my lap.

I'd take Dana wherever, whenever, and however much she'll give me. However, we're both much better than horny teenagers making out in the back of a movie theatre. I tear my lips away.

Before I can say anything, Dana reads my mind. "I want you. Take me home."

I'VE NEVER DRIVEN SO FAST. And this is LA. Everyone drives fast.

But with my pregnant girlfriend wanting in the passenger seat, begging me to pull over because she can't wait, I have no choice but to speed in order to protect everyone's dignity.

Once we make it back, we tumble up the stairs and in through the front door. "Can I have you *now*?" she hisses at me.

"Don't you want to make it to the–" Dana doesn't let me finish before she pushes me down onto the couch.

Her clothes are off in the blink of an eye; I can't seem to move fast enough. All I've done is untuck my shirt before she assists me. Strips me. She paws at the buttons of my shirt, claws at the closure of my pants. Her eyes are crazed. I've never seen her like this.

"God, I know they say pregnancy makes you horny, but–"

Dana smashes her lips against mine, her breasts glancing up against my chest. I gasp into her mouth. *Ho...ly...shit.*

I'm inside her without thinking. Dana's totally in control. Her hands lock around my wrists, pinning them against the back of the couch. The bracelet I gave her skims the inside of my forearm. Dana lifts and lowers her hips over and over, taking me as deep as she can. Every time words start to form on my lips, I'm cut off by a spark of pleasure I don't expect.

Dana's face is bent in concentration. Almost fury. Her grunts are primal. I've never seen her need it so badly.

I drop my head back, mouth ajar as needy, ragged breaths fall from my lips. "Fuck, Dana," I strain to say. "Fuck me."

Dana lifts her hips high and slams down onto my cock. My body balks with pleasure, a cry coming out of my mouth similar to if I had been punched in the gut except the feeling isn't pain. It's absolute ecstasy.

"Come, Drew. Come for me."

I fight against her grip. I want to touch her. Run my hands down the curve of her lower back, onto her hips and ass, back up onto the plane of her belly, feel her breasts and then her cheeks, pull her into a kiss and–

I don't have enough time. My body crests into pleasure. My hips roll with Dana, slower and slower, until I've released all I can.

She lifts her hips off me, the chill immediately hitting my wet cock. She drops onto the couch next to me, reaches between her legs, and starts to rub her clit fast and hard.

"Let me..."

"Shhh, Drew. Let me just–" Dana shuts her eyes. Her body freezes, hand pressing harder between her lower lips. Then, she collapses, a moan trembling from her mouth. "There. I got it. Thank you."

We mirror one another as we try to catch our breath. I start to smile and say something but stop when Dana rolls off the couch and pads into the kitchen as if nothing has happened.

What the hell is going on?

I pull on my boxers and follow her. She's standing at the sink, drinking from a glass of water. Liquid drips down her chin. "Hydration. Much deserved," I say and immediately hate myself for saying something so stupid.

Dana finishes her drink, wipes her mouth with the back of her hand, and sighs. "Yeah."

Naked, in the light of the kitchen, I can see how the shadows are different on the front of her body than they once were. "Are you alright?"

"Hm? Fine. Yeah. Just...horny."

"Yeah, it's just never been like...like *that*."

Dana blinks. Her face finally softens, closer to the woman I know. "Did I hurt you?"

"No, no. I'm not saying I didn't like it, not at all, but..." I go over to her and slide my hands through her hair. Her eyes flutter shut and her lips curl into a smile. "I just want to make sure you're okay."

"You're worried."

"Of course, I am. Always, but even more now." I place a hand on her waist. Things are going to change a lot in the next few months.

She shakes her head, pushes me away. "You don't have to worry about me. I'm good, Drew."

I stand there, a split of disappointment in my chest. Something is wrong. And she's not telling me.

Which probably means it has something to do with me. Dana tells me everything. Why would she feel the need to hide something from me unless she was afraid of what it could do to me? Or worse, do to us?

Dana has always been good at drawing things out of me with just the right question or the right phrase. I've tried to learn from her. But she's trained to do that. I'm just a novice.

The bathroom door shuts just outside the kitchen. I go to it and rest my head against the door. I know, listening to her pee, how romantic.

I can't stand to have her far from me.

The faucet turns on.

"D."

"Oh my god, Drew. You're like a cat. Or a toddler," Dana says through the bathroom door.

"Sorry."

"Give me a minute."

I swallow. I don't have a minute to give. "What if we moved in together?"

The faucet turns off. The door creaks open. Dana's brow is furrowed. "What?"

"I thought—" *Yeah, what* were *you thinking, Drew?* "The longer we have to prepare for the baby together, the easier it will be once they're here."

Dana's hand rests on the door as if she's a second away from slamming it in my face.

"Then I can be closer to you. I can take care of you."

She sighs. "Drew, you don't have to—"

"Stop. That *is* what I have to do."

Dana's face falls.

"Isn't that—don't you want that?" I ask, my voice curling out pathetically.

"Of course, I do. Just…"

Just what?

"Too fast. It's too fast for me. Right now. Let me get a handle on everything first." Dana touches my cheek. "Okay?"

This would be the moment in the movie that I tell her I love her. But I can't. I feel like my heart has been stuffed with buckshot. I can't handle another rejection right now, especially when I don't know where this hesitance and distance are coming from.

Force a smile. Remember that for all the changes you're feeling, she's feeling it tenfold. "Okay."

Dana kisses my cheek and then goes to collect her clothes.

I don't know what I did. Which means I don't know what I have to fix. And worst of all, I have no idea what any of this means for us.

23

DANA

I thought I'd be excited to walk into Oh, Baby!, our local baby superstore, but all I feel is overwhelm. Even with Harley and Gillian by my side.

"Okay, let's start with the big stuff," Gillian says, pulling me toward the displays of cribs and bassinets.

"No, let's start small. The cute things," Harley says, tugging me the other way.

"Whoa, whoa, whoa. Delicate pregnant woman here. Maybe quit it with the–" I wave their hands off me and take a deep breath. "Let's just walk around first, okay?"

Truth be told, I don't have the mental space to even consider what I might need for a baby right now. Everyone has told me I have to start preparing early because in the blink of an eye I'll be nine months pregnant and struggling to get up off the couch.

There's just...so much going on in my head right now.

"Fine, but we're taking a basket," Harley says, pulling a light blue basket out from the corral.

Gillian smiles. "*That* we can agree on."

I have to smile, remembering how the two of them used

to fight like cats and dogs. Now they're the best of mom friends. Even if they still hold each other's feet to the fire now and then.

We start down one of the aisles. Rattles, teethers, tiny stuffed animals. Things that should be making me squeal with joy and anticipation. I can't muster any excitement.

"See anything you like, Dana?" Gillian asks.

"No, not really," I reply.

"I told you the little things were too overwhelming to start with," Gillian ribs Harley, only to receive an elbow to the gut afterward.

I continue to let them lead me around the store, limiting my vocabulary to "yes", "no", "like that", "hate that".

It's the clothing section that does me in.

"Now look at this," Gillian says, picking up a tiny onesie. "Drew would just *die.*"

I crack a smile at the yellow onesie with the graphic of a smiling peach. "'Daddy's Little Peach'...what does that even mean?"

"It doesn't matter what it means. Once you're a mom, babies are comparable to food. Any food. It's a simple point of fact," Harley explains in her best radio voice.

I shuffle through the rack a little longer and stop on one I shouldn't. My face contorts.

"Please pass me to Grandma," it reads.

I pull it off the rack and stare at it. I stare hard.

"What've you got th—ohhhh..." Gillian peeks over my shoulder and recoils before she can finish her sentence.

"How is it that none of our kids will have grandmothers?" I say softly, straightening out the fabric of the onesie.

Harley and Gillian exchange a look. "I guess I never thought about that," Gillian says.

"Axel's mom is gone. Grant's mom is gone. Hunter's too. And Drew's."

"Well, our kids still *have* grandmothers," Harley corrects. "They're just not alive. But–"

"Our mother isn't dead. Do you say she's a grandmother to Stella and Tana?" I ask. I'm not trying to cause a scene or an argument. I need to know.

Harley shrugs. "She could. She just chose not to be one."

"*Harley,*" Gillian scolds.

After how Mom seemed to latch onto her after her prodigal son-esque return two years ago, I don't blame Harley. However with each passing day, all I have wanted is my mom. How can I become a mom myself if I don't have my mom to lean on? To ask questions of. To just have whisper, "Everything will be alright," and for once, *for once,* I'd believe it.

Gillian touches my shoulder. "Let's sit down."

Without realizing it, I've started shaking. *What's going on?*

Gillian leads me over to a bench (which are thankfully plentiful in a store for babies and expectant mothers). "Let's take some deep breaths."

I try to, but I can't. I shut my eyes tight. There's an aching in my chest. An emptiness.

Something I've been avoiding for a long time now. Something I haven't let myself look at.

"I'm not over it."

"Mom?" Harley asks.

I nod.

"I don't think any of us are."

"No, but–" Deep breath. "I've never had a chance to even think about it. I was so worried about all of you. You were all so dependent on me." I swallow, but it hurts. There's so much tension built up in my jaw. How long have I been holding this back? "I had to keep it together for all of you. I don't think I've ever even cried..." I stop. My eyes ache with unshed tears. "I've never even cried over her leaving."

And right there in fucking Oh, Baby! the tears come trembling down my cheeks. Huge sobs. No one likes crying in public, but in a venue such as this, I doubt anyone would question it.

Gillian wraps her arms around me and lets me go to town, soaking her shoulder with my salty tears. I feel Harley's hand on my shoulder. "We're sorry, Dana."

"Yeah, really sorry."

I want to tell them they don't have to be sorry. It was never their fault. I wanted to be everything for them. I *wanted* to take care of them. But no words come out, just choked weeping.

The person who owes me an apology is our mother and the fucked up thing is, I'd never demand that of her. I just want her back. I want her to be the mom she was when I was just a little girl and she was tucking me in at night. I want to smell her, that specific smell mothers have that only their children can identify them by. I want to cry on her shoulder, want to celebrate my life with her, I want...

I want my mom.

But at the same time I *don't* want my mother. I guess I just want to be able to know what it would feel like to be going through this with *a* mom who cares.

"Here." Gillian hands me a tissue.

I dab at my eyes and blow my nose, suddenly overcome with mortification as I glance around the store and see people shopping, trying to mind their own business. "Sorry. I didn't mean to."

"It's okay, we both know how emotional it can get. Trust me," Harley says with a small chuckle.

"And you want to do this again?" I say incredulously.

Harley laughs. "It ends up being worth it. Trust me."

"Trust *us*," Gillian says, squeezing my arms.

I do.

Gillian's loving smile falters. She turns her eyes away from me. "Dana, this might be a bad time, but since we're here..."

My stomach drops.

"I think you should know that Willow has been saying some awful stuff about Drew."

I nod slowly. "She said as much to me."

"When?!" Harley asks. Clearly, she's more in the know than I am.

"She found me in the parking lot after our lunch the other day."

Harley's face twists. "That's so fucking creepy."

"Why didn't you tell us?!"

The reason I didn't tell my sisters was because I need to find out the truth for myself. I don't want them to start looking at Drew differently. I want to get the full truth, make it totally clear before getting the wild and fiery tempers of the Solace girls involved. "Because...well, I know you're friends with her–"

Gillian scoffs. "Not friends. Not anymore. She's..." She shakes her head. "Something is going on with her."

I sigh. "That's what I was afraid of."

"She's always been a little off, but lately it's gotten to the point we're worried about her. But she won't accept any help. And we can't sit there and just wait for her to finally accept that she needs some serious professional help," Gillian explains. "So, Lola confronted her about the stuff she's been saying and, to make a long story short, we're cutting her out."

I smile. "You'd really do that for me?"

Gillian looks at me like I'm crazy. "You're my sister. Duh."

"Plus, she never liked Willow anyway."

"*Harley.*"

I laugh and let myself nestle into the spot between my two sisters. I might not have my mom, but I can always feel safe around them. And that means the world to me.

"Whatever she said to you, I wouldn't take it seriously. Willow will do anything to get her way. She's always been that way. And now that something has gone unhinged, well, there's no telling what she'll do," Gillian explains.

There's still so much I don't know. And haven't talked to Drew about.

"Come on. Let's get back to the cute stuff, shall we?" Harley says.

While Gillian and Harley try to keep me distracted, my mind is racing. Maybe Willow is truly willing to do whatever she can to ruin my relationship and get Drew back. However, I am in the job of emotions. I know people don't just do things out of thin air.

There's a story here. I need to know about those texts. I need to know about the night Drew's mom died.

And I need to know about his father too.

I need the truth. I need it now. And I need it from Drew.

24

DREW

I watch as the 3D printer slides back and forth as it constructs the latest part of the engine. This sucker has been one of my favorite investments. Now I don't have to go into the office to work on my models, I can do it all from the comfort of my home.

It's still going to take some time before this next piece will be ready, so I return to the model as it stands. About halfway done. No need for any more tinkering, but I can't help myself removing a piece and putting it back in.

This will work. It has to.

A wave of déjà vu hits me. I don't like it. Because it reminds me of a person I try desperately not to think about.

My father.

If there's one thing I can say he gave to me, it was my love of building things. Those were the only good times we had, building model airplanes and doing puzzles together. Those were the moments I believed he would stay.

A memory hits me then.

We were in the middle of a model submarine. It only had a few more pieces to go. I was still clumsy at eight years old and unable to handle the glue with the necessary finesse. Dad was there to glue the pieces together.

The only time he was really there.

A tear falls down my face, blurring the model engine in front of me.

I've always been afraid of turning into him.

But now I know. *I know.*

I won't be anything like him. I won't walk out on my child or the woman I love. Because if my child loves me half as much as I loved and adored my father, my father who didn't give a single shit about actually *being* a father, then I know that is not a love worth betraying.

And Dana...

I've wanted her for so long. Now I have her. Why would I fuck that up?

My phone starts buzzing on my worktable. Speak of the devil (or the angel, really).

"Hey, I was just thinking about you," I answer, taking a seat on my rolling stool I use to traverse my home office.

"Where are you?" Her voice sounds strained.

"I'm at home. Why? What's wrong?" My body locks up. "Are you okay? Is something wrong with the baby?"

"No, no, it's not that." Dana goes quiet for a moment. "We just need to talk about some things, Drew."

My heart, which had lodged in my throat with worry, now plummets into my stomach. I know what "we need to talk" means. But I can't come to grips with the possibility that Dana is casting me out of her life. Not now.

"Okay," I say, but my voice comes out like a puff of smoke. "I'm just working. Feel free to drop by whenever."

"Thank you. I'll see you soon."

"Sounds good."

I hang up and stare at my phone in my hand. The

printer groans in the background. There's no way I'm going to get any more work done. My focus is shot. I just have to bide my time. I don't even know how far away Dana is. She could be twenty minutes; she could be half an hour. Fucking LA traffic makes everything unpredictable.

My cheeks feel hot. My heart throbs.

I need a cold shower.

I go upstairs to my bedroom; as I pass my dresser on my way to the bathroom, something red catches my eye. It's a little box that's been sitting there for years now. Ever since Mom passed away. I've never brought myself to open it.

Until now.

I pop open the ring box and look at my mother's ring. My father might have been a deadbeat, but he bought my mother a pretty nice engagement ring. Or should I say *promise* ring. They were never married. Once dad was fully out of the picture, she started wearing it on her right hand.

It's beautiful. Gold band, a diamond punctuated with two more little ones on the sides. Must have cost him a pretty penny.

"Keep it," Mom insisted. "I want you to have it. There's no use putting me in the ground with it."

The conversations you end up having with a dying relative are some of the strangest. Discussions of mortality became so common place when we knew we had to plan for her end.

I, of course, followed her wishes. She didn't say it explicitly, but I knew it was meant for the woman she hoped I would one day marry.

I'm not going to wait any longer. Dana's going to know how much I want her. If she's scared I'm not going to commit, I'm going to allay all of her fears. I have a ring for her and three words that have been waiting just behind my lips to let her know how much I care for her.

Regardless of the conversation she's coming here to have, I'm ready to give her all of me.

I take a shower, the cold water shocking me to my core. Resetting my body was the exact thing I needed to do. My pulse slows down, my body temperature returns to normal. I'm ready.

As I get out of the shower, I hear someone in my room. "Dana?" I call out. It's not unusual for her to let herself in. And if she heard the water running, she would come right up here.

There's no response.

"Just give me a second," I call out. I wrap my towel around my waist and enter the bedroom. I freeze in my tracks.

It's not Dana.

It's Willow.

She's facing away from me, toward the dresser. "It's beautiful, Drew." She turns around slowly, revealing my mother's ring on her finger.

I immediately feel a fight response coming on. That ring is not for her. Was *never* meant for her. "How did you get in here?"

"Most girls would say we're moving too fast, but not me," she says, ignoring my question. Willow smiles widely. "Yes. I'll marry you."

"What the fuck are you on?"

She laughs. "You're so funny."

God, she really is not well. I can see it in her eyes. They're sort of glazed over as if she's not even really here. "Willow, you're sick."

"Lovesick. Sure." She continues to look at the ring.

Hypnotized. "I knew you'd come to your senses and pick me over her. I just knew it."

I go toward her and reach out for her wrist. "Give that back. It's not for–"

Willow twists into my grip and grabs me by the back of the head, forcing her lips onto mine. I try to tear away, but all it does is throw me off balance. Willow takes advantage of this, pushing me back onto the bed. She straddles my hips, pressing herself into my crotch. I'm trying to keep the towel closed, but her wild movement is making it hard. "Let's celebrate, Drew." She lowers her mouth to my ear. "Like we used to."

My eyes widen. Holy shit, she's about to–"Willow, don't do this."

"I love when you beg." Her hand trails up the inside of my thigh.

We're interrupted by a voice. "What the hell do you think you're doing?"

Dana.

In her distraction, Willow lets up just enough so I can shove her off me. Willow yelps as she rolls off the bed. I scramble off the bed and across the room, tightening my towel again. "Dana, I promise, this isn't–"

Dana doesn't even look at me or wait for an explanation. She stalks over to Willow. "Leave. *Now.*"

"Or what?"

Dana holds up her phone. "I've already got 9-1-1 typed out. You want to deal with me or the cops?"

Willow pushes herself back up to her feet and lunges toward Dana. "He invited me here."

"If you even think about getting violent, consider the police already on their way," Dana says, ducking out of the way.

I take a few steps toward them, but fear is sharp in my chest. "I didn't invite her, Dana. I–"

"He wants me. He's playing games with you."

"Dana, I swear, it's–"

"I saw you walking around the property looking for a way in," Dana barks at Willow. Her hazel eyes are eclipsed with fire. "My car was parked right across the street." She looks to me apologetically. "I'm sorry I didn't come earlier. I wasn't sure if you two were–"

I frown. So that's what all of this is about. Some suspicion that I might have been unfaithful. "No, Dana. It's alright."

"I showed you those texts!"

"What texts?" I hiss.

"We got coffee! You wanted to see me!" Willow cries out desperately. She's getting more pathetic by the moment.

"You were sending me unsolicited nudes and I met up with you to tell you to back off! You're fucking..." I stop and take a deep breath. I'm not going to call her names. She doesn't deserve that. She deserves a mental institution.

Dana sighs with relief. "That settles that, then."

"You were with me the night your mom died," Willow screams, a last ditch effort. "You love me more than–than–"

"I didn't love you, I was just an asshole," I cry out in response. My mother had never wanted her illness to take over my life. That was a near impossibility. But that night, she wanted me to go out and be with my friends. With my girlfriend. "I'd promised to visit her the day before and, yes, I didn't. I fucked up. But no one knew she was going to die that night. It all just–" I shake my head. "Dana, you have to know I regret it more than–"

"You never have to explain yourself to me, Drew," Dana says in her usual even tone. She smiles. And despite everything, I smile too. She's choosing me. "Willow, I'm afraid your time is up. Do I need to make the call or–"

Willow screams. It's a scary sound, curdling spit and shredding throat. She pulls at her own dark hair and turns to run out of the room.

But Dana runs after her, grabbing her arm harshly. "You're not going anywhere with *that* on your finger."

I rush to the open door to make sure Willow doesn't make a break for it. She looks between Dana and me like a wounded animal before taking off the ring and dropping it on the floor. "You two are doomed. He'll never love you like he loved me. You'll see, he'll be crawling back to me in no time."

Dana shakes her head. "Come on, Willow. I'll walk you out."

I step aside and let the two women pass. Dana is some sort of superhero in this moment. The woman doesn't seem to know fear like I do. As she passes me, she smiles knowingly.

We'll talk, I think I hear her mind say.

I watch them go down the stairs and then turn back into the room, picking the ring up off the ground. I hold it up at eye level.

If I was decided before, then I'm fucking resolved as steel.

Dana will be mine. Forever.

25

———

DANA

I lied to Willow.

Adrenaline has been coursing through my veins since the second I pulled up in front of Drew's house and I saw Willow at the front door, her hand on her hip. I thought I'd caught him in the act. So brazen as to have his lover over when he knew I was also on my way.

But when I saw her start peering inside, I knew something was amiss.

Further confirmed once she wriggled through an open window.

The second I watched her go in, I called the police and told them to come, but to keep the sirens out and stay out of sight because the woman was crazy and I had no idea if she was armed or not.

I couldn't just stay there and do nothing until they came, so I went inside.

I'm glad they listened, though, and as I walk out of the house, a squad car is stopping in front of the house. The officers come to us and after clearing up who is who, they take her kicking and screaming to the station.

I watch them go before I walk back inside and shut the door behind me, turning every lock possible. I rest my head against the door and take a deep breath. I have no question that the woman will try everything in her power to escape and come for us again, but at least for now we should be safe.

Two hands land on my shoulders. I jump and nearly tear myself out of Drew's grasp. "Oh, my god. You scared me," I whisper.

His hands tighten. "I'm sorry."

Drew, now clothed in an obvious rush, turns me to face him. I can see the aftermath of anxiety all over his face. Eyes wide, lips pressed into a thin line. "Are you okay?"

I nod. "Yeah. You?"

"Thanks to you, yeah." Drew's gaze falls and he tries to smile. "You really mama-beared that whole situation."

"Oh, my god. The baby." My hands fly to my stomach. It's not often the baby is far from my mind. But something about this whole situation gave me tunnel vision. I had to fight for Drew. For us. I guess in a way that was fighting for the baby too. "What if–oh god, what if she had–"

Drew pulls me into his embrace. "Shhh...It's okay. You're safe. We're safe now, baby. All three of us."

I melt into his arms, my breath trembling. God, the stress of this day won't end, will it?

Drew kisses the side of my head. "I'm here, alright? Just hold onto me. I'm here."

I don't know how long I cling to Drew. But, *fuck*, do I cling onto him. He is my rock. My everything. And now that I know this was all some misunderstanding tainted by the ramblings of a mad woman, I can breathe easy again, knowing my man is *mine*.

"Let me make you a cup of tea, huh?" Drew finally asks.

I let him guide me into the kitchen. He sits me down on a stool as if I'm a tender, fragile creature. Tucks my hair behind my ear. Kisses my forehead.

I love this man so much.

Drew clears his throat as he puts water in the kettle. "Now you know about the night my mom died."

I look over at him.

"You must think I'm awful."

I shake my head. "No, Drew. I think you're human."

He looks up at me, the blues of his eyes taut and strained. "You're kinder to me than I deserve."

"You deserve the world, Drew."

He begins to rebut but stops himself. "I know I'm not going to win this one."

I finally smile, humming out a tiny laugh.

"So, you knew about the texts," he says and puts the kettle on the stove. "Is that what you were coming over to talk about?"

My shoulders fall. "Why didn't you tell me she was bothering you? By the way, we have to stop by the police station to press charges. Willow needs to get help."

"We will. And I didn't tell you because it didn't have to be your problem. There's already so much else on your plate."

"But if you had told me, I wouldn't have had to worry. I wouldn't have had to even question what was going on."

Drew leans against the counter, crossing his arms over his chest. "I'm sorry, Dana. I'm not the best at saying everything on my mind. You know that. Better than anyone, probably."

I remain quiet. And Drew doesn't speak either. The only noises in the kitchen eventually become the whistling of the kettle, the knocking of a mug on the counter, the shuffling of tea leaves into the strainer.

Drew sets the mug in front of me and sits down. I watch as the tea begins to steep, the water growing darker by the minute. The smell of Darjeeling is intoxicating. I take Drew's hand and place it in my lap. "If we're doing this, Drew, really doing this, baby and all, you can't keep things like that from me."

"I'm sorry, D. Really, I am."

"I know."

More quiet. The tea steam starts to lessen enough that I can actually take a sip. "It hurts too much to know more than everyone else does."

Drew's thumb slides across my skin. "What do you mean?"

Deep breath, Dana. You can say it. The entire drive here, my thoughts of Drew were interspliced with thoughts of my mother. And everything that she put my sisters and me through. "I knew about Mom. Maybe even before the others."

"That she was...cheating on your father?" Drew asks carefully.

I shake my head. "Not in so many words. No. But I could feel her growing further away long before she actually disappeared. It was years of her distance."

"Oh, Dana, I'm so sorry."

I bite my lower lip. "When Dad was working and Mom was alone, she was distant. I was left to take care of my sisters. Her mind was somewhere else completely. And when Dad came home, she was the woman we all knew and loved. Bright and loving. I don't know if it was guilt eating her alive or if she just never wanted to be a mother in the first place, but—"

"That's not true. You know it. There are five of you, for heaven's sake."

I shake my head. "I think it's easy to get lost in motherhood. To wonder what you are outside of it. Mom had five children in her twenties. She never even had a job even though she managed to get her college degree. All of it hung on Dad's shoulders. Then we got older and needed her less. At least, that's what she must have thought."

"But you always need your mom...always..." Drew whispers.

Our eyes meet. I smile. "Yes, you know that well."

"I do."

I touch his cheek softly. The beard is in need of a trim. But I don't mind it. "I felt like my mother had gone long before she actually left. Does that make sense?"

He nods. "That must have been so hard."

My eyes pinch with tears. *Not again...* "It was. It was so h-hard."

I've done way more weeping today than I've done probably my entire adult life. If this is a sign of times to come, I am going to need to invest in Kleenex stock.

Drew takes my hand and kisses my fingertips as I cry. Such an intimate, close gesture. I want him to kiss every part of my body and I don't mean it sexually (although that wouldn't be so bad either). I want him to appreciate every tender part of me. To love *all* of me despite the ugliness.

"You didn't deserve that, Dana."

"I know, but it's my t-trauma. I have to live with it. And be good despite it."

"You never have to be anything but what you are with me."

"God, why do you always say the right things?" I say through a laugh that's also sort of a sob.

Drew wipes my tears away. "I had a very good teacher." Gingerly, he kisses my lips, then presses his forehead to mine.

My tears abate, finally. I am grounded again. Here with Drew. Father of my baby. The man I love.

"I love you," I whisper.

"I love you too," he says back without hesitation.

It is not a dramatic declaration. No boomboxes held overhead or tearful explanations in the rain. It is simple. It is easy.

It's *us*.

He pulls the ring out of his pocket and holds it up. "Not a proposal. Not yet. I know you said you don't want things to move too fast just because we did everything backwards, but..."

I resist the urge to say that I would accept a proposal right here on the spot. Old Dana didn't know what she was talking about. New Dana wants to be Drew Young's forever and ever.

"I want you to have this. As a promise. That I'll always be here for you. For our baby."

I smile.

"My father walked out on me without explanation. I've never been able to talk about it with you. With anyone, really. But I still remember the last time I saw him. The last time we talked. I was eight years old."

His eyes take on a faraway look.

"We had been building a model submarine for a few hours. Just the two of us. It was our thing. Suddenly, Dad said, 'I think we're out, kid,' squeezing the glue bottle with all his might. It wheezed angrily, glue sputtering across our cardboard workstation.

"'Oh, that's okay. We can stop for today,' I said. I was

always a particularly understanding child. I had to be when my dad kept leaving and waltzing back into my life, looking for forgiveness.

"Dad looked at me, his eyes reflecting my own. And a look passed over his face that I'll never forget. A frown and then a half-smile and then... 'No, I'll go get some now,' he said getting to his feet and starting toward the door. I scrambled after him. 'Wait, don't go!' I pleaded.

"'I'm just going to the store, Drew. I'll be right back.'" His eyes are on the floor.

"Any time Dad left, I assumed it would be for the last time. It didn't matter how many promises he made to Mom and me. He'd left so many times, even when she was pregnant. God. I begged him to stay. To let me go with him, but he wouldn't let me. He just grabbed his leather jacket off the hall tree and slid it on, ignoring my plea. 'Tell your mother I'll be back, alright?'

"I stopped dead in my tracks. I'd heard that before. That meant he wouldn't be back. At least not for a while." He closes his eyes. Pain clear on his face. My heart breaks for the man he is and the little boy he was.

"His reasons for leaving were never clear. I could never determine his patterns. Sometimes, it would be fights that would drive him away. Other times it was only a decision."

He took in a deep breath.

"'He always had a restless heart. You can't tame someone like that, you just can't,' my mother once said to me about my father. We didn't know where he went or what he did. As I got older, Mom and I would sometimes guess. We'd make up grandiose stories about what trouble my father could be getting into. To cope.

"'I bet he's strung up on a flagpole by his underwear,' she said once. 'I bet he's just lost his last dime to a bag of cocaine that's actually powdered sugar,' was my suggestion. That always made her laugh. And as long as we could laugh about him being gone, we couldn't cry."

His eyes move to mine. "That night, I remember looking down at the floor by the door, feeling my father's eyes on me. I silently begged him to hug me. To please let me know he loved me."

A tear escapes my eye. Poor boy. How hard it must have been to go through that not just once but time and time again, never knowing if the man who was supposed to take care of him, love him, would ever return.

"But he didn't. He barely even said goodbye. And that was the last time I ever saw him. After years of in and out and in and out, he'd finally chosen out."

His head shaking, he said, "My father was a liar who knew nothing about love. Knew nothing about accepting it. Or giving it, for that matter. The last time he returned, he'd promised and promised that he wouldn't leave. That he was ready to put down roots. That we'd go on a family vacation. That he'd take my mother on a proper date for the first time in god knew how long.

"Instead, he walked out.

"Mom offered to help me with the model sub. We did finish it. But a week later, I smashed it on the sidewalk. I was so angry at him."

His head falls down to his chest. "But you know what the worst part is? I was afraid you might think I'm like him, but–"

"No, Drew. Never."

"Really?"

"Really. If I believed that even for a second, I'd have to believe I'm like my mom, and I know I'm nothing like her.

We are better. It's their loss, but we can learn from their mistakes."

He massages the ring finger on my left hand. "Good. Still, though, the promise remains. Regardless of what happens between us, I'm here for you. You'll always be my best friend. And I'll always be the best father I can be to our child."

I let him slide the ring onto my hand. "Fits perfect."

"Meant to be. Maybe. I don't know."

I giggle and clasp his hands in mine. "I like the sound of that."

Drew flushes.

"And...I promise to tell you when things are bothering me. And to trust you first and foremost. No matter what."

"Good. Because I haven't had a crush on you for years just to get into a relationship with you and cheat on you."

I laugh. "Well, that's good to know."

Drew kisses my cheek. "If you need me to remind you, just say the word. Because I'll remind you again..." He kisses my other cheek. "And again..." My chin. "And again..."

Soon enough, he's peppering kisses across my face, neck, and collarbone. I feel my body swaying toward him closer and closer until I'm off the stool and in his arms, thirsting for his lips to caress me over and over.

"If we moved in together..." I say through a pleasured sigh.

Drew hums against my skin.

"We should move in here. Your place is nicer."

He laughs and lifts his head, brown hair falling into his eyes. "You want to move in with me, D?"

"I think we could be okay roommates."

"Roommates, huh?" He laughs and runs his thumb

tenderly under my lip. God, he's sexy. "Then why don't we go break in your new bedroom, huh?"

Drew throws me over his shoulder; I laugh the whole way up the stairs, back to the bedroom. I've slept here many times, been with him in his bed before. But this time is wholly different.

Drew drops me on the bed carefully and spreads my legs. "Lay back. I'm going to take care of you."

His kissing continues, this time from my ankle all the way up to the inside of my thigh. He captures my underwear in his teeth and pulls them down my legs, with the aid of his hands. I let out a tremoring breath.

"You're already dripping for me," he says in a ragged voice, breath brushing up against my center.

"Do something about it, then," I reply.

Drew smiles, a devilish look in his eye. He kisses my lower lips gently, brushing back my pubic hair. He presses his nose into it and takes in a deep breath. "Mmm...mine. All mine." His hand slides up to my belly. I put mine over it, a warm beam of connection through me as we acknowledge what's growing inside me.

His tongue darts into me and begins to tease and lap up my juices. I'm in heaven. No rushing, just enjoying, allowing the waves of pleasure to wash over me as if I'm lying in the warm tide of the ocean.

"Love this. Love you," he groans before kissing my hips bone.

I wrap my hands around his head and guide him upward until his lips are on mine and I can taste my own ambrosia. Drew's hips move side to side, aiding me as I pull his shorts down, releasing his length. It leans up against my belly. I giggle.

"What?" he asks breathlessly.

I capture his eyes with mine for a long moment. "I'm just thinking about the first time."

Drew's look of interrupted passion melts, giving way to a wistful smile. "Thank god I walked in on you naked, huh?"

I stroke the side of his face.

"Or should I say thank *you* for being a horny little devil that day," he says, capturing my ear lobe in his teeth.

I laugh all the way until I feel him pressing his hips forward to meet mine, sliding his cock inside. "Go slow," I whisper as my body unfurls, tension still held over from confronting Willow.

"Of course."

I guide my hips up to his over and over, letting myself stretch, until the pinching sensation is gone and all that's left is a warm pool of pleasure. I sigh in ecstasy as he fills me.

"So beautiful," he whispers through swollen lips.

I tighten my legs around him, bringing him further inside. Drew's breath seizes and then he laughs.

"Fuck, you feel so good."

"It's like you were always meant to be here."

I hear him swallow. "Yeah. Exactly like that."

From there, any ability to speak is lost. Our hips rev together, again and again. A communion of everything we've built.

Because it's not just the mess of the past four months. It's the years of friendship, of connection. We've worked so hard. We've earned this.

This...happiness.

I'm rutting hard and fast, the movements almost not my own, controlled by some higher power. Pleasure is close to boiling over. Tears start to poke at my eyes.

Burning with euphoria. They spill over just before I tip over the edge.

"Yes," I whisper with the last bit of clarity I have before the orgasm takes me away.

My body seizes, rising up to meet Drew's. I wrap myself around him as tightly as I can, groaning with release. The tears spill too.

Drew joins me not long after. I clench around him, welcoming him inside. He sighs against my cheek, kisses my tears away, softly cooing some encouraging words I can't quite make out in my haze.

It doesn't matter what the words are, though. Drew is here, with me, in my arms.

We lay here, tangled together on the bed, Drew's fingers trailing up and down my side. He pauses each time he brushes my waist. Always complemented by a creeping smile.

I tuck some of his sweaty hair back. "You're going to make a great daddy."

Drew's eyes widen. "You think?"

I nuzzle his cheek. "I *know*."

"Thanks."

He threads his fingers through mine and pulls our clasped hands into the air. The ring twinkles like a star in the sky. I haven't even realized how the room has darkened around us in the twilight hours.

"Mine, mine, mine," Drew mutters, then kisses the ring.

The day has been too long. And I could fall asleep right here in Drew's arms feeling safe and loved, forever.

But...

"I'm starving," I say against his neck.

"Oh, I bet you are, mama." Drew trails kisses down to my stomach and lingers there with a smile. "Can't have you hungry." He gets up out of bed (to my disappointment) and starts to prowl for his phone. "What are you in the mood for? Tacos? Pasta?" He spots the phone on the dresser and starts to type around. "Both? Or something else?"

I can only smile as I watch him type on his phone. Already trying to take care of me and our family.

Drew looks at me. "Anything sound good?"

My smile spreads into a grin. "All of it."

WITH BELLIES full of both tacos and pasta, we retreat to bed together again, love drunk and exhausted from the trials of the day. To think just a few hours ago, I was questioning Drew's commitment to me.

Now, I'm in his bed while he strokes the gentle curve of my stomach, his mouth resting against my skin, talking softly to our baby.

"I know you can't understand me yet."

I laugh.

"You've still got a few weeks to go before that."

I stroke his hair softly and smile, letting my eyes flutter shut. I feel so lucky that the man I love is so invested in our baby's growth. Drew hasn't looked away from our pregnancy for a second. Which leads me to believe it was never a mistake. Not really. How can something so full of love be labeled an accident?

"But I can't resist."

I rest my hand over Drew's, the one that curves the slightest bit over my changing form. It's only going to get stranger by the day, watching myself shift to grow a whole human inside of me.

I wouldn't trade it, though. Not for the world.

"I love you, little D."

"Little *D*?!" I ask incredulously.

"Yeah! Our names are both D names, so our baby has to have a D name too, don't you think?" Drew says, hapless smile on his lips.

I roll my eyes. "That sounds like we're on some sitcom from the nineteen fifties."

"Yeah, I love it."

I sigh into the pillow. This is not a conversation I am willing to have right now, when I'm in a food coma. Names can come later. For now, I relish Drew's ongoing monologue to our baby who can't yet hear it.

"You won't have to worry about a thing, baby. Because Daddy loves you and Mommy loves you." Drew grins at me. "And Mommy loves Daddy."

"And Daddy loves Mommy, don't forget that part."

He kisses my stomach once more and then slides up next to me. "Oh, would never. *Could* never." Drew presses his lips to mine. Long, unflinching. A far cry from what we were when we began, hiding our passion from the light of day.

Now we have all the time in the world.

"So, when should I move in?" I say just as I'm about to drift off to sleep in his arms.

Drew pushes his face into my neck. "How about tomorrow?"

With a smile, I drift off to sleep, with dreams of the guest room turning into a nursery and our little one safely asleep down the hall while we embrace in the joyful exhaustion that is our future as parents.

26

DREW

Holidays are the hardest without my mom. Birthdays too. No matter how many people I'm surrounded by, no matter how much fun I could possibly have, her absence is felt in the deepest part of me.

However, the grief is a little lighter this Easter. My first one as a host.

First, because I got a call yesterday telling me that Willow has been forcefully committed to an asylum.

We thought it was better to protect ourselves against her by getting a restraining order and maybe court mandatory help for her, so we pressed charges against her the day after her attack. We went down to the station and gave them our statements. She was being kept in lockdown for forty-eight hours while they investigated what had happened.

Apparently, while she was there, she had a psychotic break. They say it was bad and she had to be heavily sedated.

They aren't letting her out anytime soon, I was told, and even after that, she'll have to answer to breaking and entering, attempted rape, and kidnapping, as well as stalking me and Dana. But the police officer who called was pretty sure she was there for life or at least for a loooong time. Which is a relief. We were watching our backs for a while there, for her payback, but I guess we can just live our lives now without having that extra worry.

I asked the nice officer to please let us know if she is ever released so we can then be on the lookout, and he said they would, so there is that.

But more importantly, I've graduated from the adult that tags along to celebrations to the one having the celebration myself. That's growth if I've ever heard it.

"Okay, ready...set..." Dana calls out as if she's talking to a whole classroom of kids rather than just Jessica, Stella, and Tana. "Go!"

Jessica and Stella tear off while Tana hobbles on her feet hand in hand with Harley and Grant who are hunched over and cooing excitedly to her about spotting easter eggs. Hard to believe she's just over a year old and getting her feet under her like this. Time flies.

I look over at Dana who is smiling ear to ear, watching her nieces search for the eggs. We spent a good chunk of this morning finding the perfect places to stick eggs all over the yard. "They can't be too obvious but they can't be too hard to find either," she instructed.

Stella and Jessica are already heading toward the backyard, their baskets full, the two of them laughing. Gillian follows, making sure they don't get themselves into trouble. Tana has settled on the grass where we left some out in the open for her. She's trying desperately to suck on a purple egg that Harley keeps pulling out of her reach.

"This is what we have to look forward to, huh?" I murmur to Dana.

She smiles and slides her hands down over her stomach, showing off the contour of her tiny bump. Every morning, she stands in the mirror, saddened she hasn't popped yet. "Don't get too ahead of yourself, Drew," Dana says.

I rest my hand over hers. "Trust me, I'm not." I plant a small kiss on her lips and brush my nose against hers.

"It's so cute I may vomit," Amy exclaims.

We pull away from each other. Force of habit. I keep my hand on Dana's waist and draw her back into me. While the kids search for eggs, us adults congregate into a little group. The gang is all here: Amy and Hunter, Gillian and Axel, Kira, Kent, and, unprecedently, Victoria made it back from a project in Brazil in time for the holiday. You wouldn't even know she came straight from the airport from how put together she looks.

"Are you all settled in yet, Dana?" Hunter asks, his eyes following Jessica as she carefully tiptoes through a bed of greenery.

"I would be if Drew let me actually do any of the heavy lifting," she grumbles.

I scoff. "What kind of boyfriend would I be if I let my pregnant girlfriend move herself into my house?"

Dana ignores me. "We're trying to make sure I actually unpack, so we're only doing a few boxes at a time."

"At this rate, you'll be moved in by Christmas," Kira says.

"Much sooner than that," I say firmly. "Much, much, much."

Victoria looks up at the house with a placid, supermodel smile. I don't know what a supermodel smile *is*, but it's the one Victoria wears at all times. "You think it's big enough for you three?"

My heart flutters at being described as a trio. For the rest of my life, there will be the three of us. I can't wait.

"For now," Dana answers.

I do a double take. "For *now?*"

She laughs, hooking her arm in mine. "Well, there's only two bedrooms. If we want to have guests, they're going to have to take the couch."

"Don't be cagey, Dana," Amy says with a sly smile. "We know what you're really getting at."

"Oh, stop that," Dana hushes her sister.

I look at Kira with a raised eyebrow while Amy and Dana start to squabble. She chuckles and shakes her head. "She has four sister, Drew. You didn't really think you'd be getting away with having just one kid, did you?"

My head feels like my brain has disappeared, a lightness dizzying me. Only for a moment. "Let me get my bearings with one first, huh?"

Kira snickers and grabs me by the shoulder. "You got it."

In theory, I'd give Dana anything. In practice, thinking about another baby before this one is even earthside makes me feel faint. One thing at a time.

As if Dana can read my mind, she grabs my arm and whispers in my ear, "Don't listen to her. The house is perfect."

It is a pretty perfect house. I bought it when I finally became a lead at my company. I never anticipated sharing it with someone else, let alone Dana. Let alone the baby I'm having *with* Dana. It will serve its purpose.

But Dana's right. Someday soon, we should find a place for *us*. A house we choose together to raise our family in. Not my bachelor pad.

"Who's that?" Victoria asks, looking over her sunglasses toward the street.

We follow her gaze toward a black car that I would have to sell my soul to the devil for by the looks of how expensive it is.

Kent quirks his eyebrow. "Expecting more company, Drew?"

"Oh, *shit*," Kira says in a whisper.

The driver gets out of the car and opens the back passenger door. A familiar dark-haired man steps out. I think I've met him. Wynters, right? Has a weird first name. What is it?

"Is that Orlie?" Dana murmurs, trying to get Kira's attention.

Right. Orlie Wynters. I met him only briefly when Hunter invited all us guys to join him at his private social club last summer. He seemed nice enough if you believe ice cubes have personality traits.

Kira straightens up and clears her throat as Orlie approaches. He's in a full suit and tie, holding a manilla folder, sunglasses shielding his eyes.

"Well, that's a tall glass of water, huh?" Victoria says.

I see Kent's body stiffen and his cheeks go red.

"Did you...invite him?" I ask Kira.

She puts on an irritated smile and says through clenched teeth, "No, of course I didn't invite my robot of a boss to the family Easter, *Drew*."

I look at Dana with wide eyes. She pats my arm gingerly. "Stressed."

"Hi, Orlie. What are you doing here?" Kira says.

"Pardon me for interrupting," Orlie says in a voice so deep it makes me seem like I haven't even hit puberty yet. "Ricks, good to see you." He nods toward Hunter.

Hunter nods too. "Wynters." Ah, the strange familiarity of men in business. So withholding for no reason at all.

"I see you're having some festivities, and I–"

"It's Easter," Kira interrupts. "Do you celebrate?"

He frowns and then looks at his smartwatch. "Ah. I suppose it is. Then I'm doubly sorry for interrupting."

This guy is such a workaholic he doesn't even know when major holidays are? Yeesh.

"I have some contracts that need signing by end of day. Forgive me for the intrusion," he explains, then holds the folder out to Kira.

Kira is red in the face. I can't tell if it's from shame, anger, or something else entirely. She opens the folder and scans the documents. "You got a–"

Before she can even finish what she's saying, Orlie whips out a pen from his jacket pocket. I'm sure I'd have to sell my soul for that pen too.

"Thank you," Kira grumbles.

We all watch as she goes through the documents, Orlie occasionally pointing out where to sign. It's awkward, especially with the thrilling laugh of children in the background. When we can no longer take the silence, Kent pipes up. "Say, Orlie, why don't you stick around? I'm sure we can fit another chair at the table. And if I know Dana, she's made the best Easter dinner you could possibly imagine."

"I had a lot of help," she says with a sheepish smile my way.

"I was just the sous chef; she was the brains of the operation." After all, I can barely make a cookie without setting off the smoke alarm.

Orlie appraises each of us individually before lowering his gaze back to the contract. "Thank you for the offer, but I'm afraid I have a flight to catch."

"Work or pleasure?" Kent says with a half-smile.

"Work," Kira answers on behalf of Orlie as if they're some old married couple. She slaps the folder shut and then realizes what she's done. "Um, I mean, sorry, I just assumed."

Orlie takes the folder. Is that the beginning of a smile on his lips? The tight curve right at the corner? Or maybe it's just a figment of my imagination. A guy like that doesn't smile unless he's being held against his will and tickled. "You'd be correct in your assumption, Kira. Thank you."

"Where you off to?" Kent continues.

Kira whips around toward him, a sneer on her lips. *Quit it.*

Note to future self: don't ask too many questions of my child's friends or acquaintances in order to not receive wrath.

"Business in China. Will be back by Wednesday."

"Now, that's quite a turnaround! You don't even do that, do you, Vic?" Kent says, his brown eyes glowing as they take in Victoria.

"All part of the job," Orlie says with a tight nod. I wonder what's behind those dark sunglasses. Black holes of capitalism maybe. He clears his throat. "Anyway, let me offer an apology once more for my intrusion. Have a happy...holiday."

Everyone says their goodbyes, except for Kira who stares after him as he retreats to the car.

"Poor driver has to work on easter," Amy mutters.

"Not everyone celebrates Easter, Amy," Dana says.

The youngest Solace rolls her eyes. "Wow, I had no idea."

Once the car pulls down the street, we all wait for Kira's reaction. She remains nonplussed. Or tries to. "Why are you all looking at me?"

"That was..." Dana looks to me. I look back, unsure how to give her the word she's trying to find. "Odd."

"Odd. That's a good way to put it," Kent says.

Kira waves her hand through the air. "You're being dramatic. I'm sorry if it interrupted your holiday."

"That's not why it was weird!" Amy says. "It was just...*weird.*"

"Wow, you're a writer, right?" Kira jabs back.

"I'm just saying there was tension. Wouldn't you all agree?"

We nervously exchange looks around the circle. Clearly, we all agree. But are any of us willing to poke Kira the bear any further? Definitely not.

"Whatever," Kira mumbles.

"Daddy! I got an egg full of quarters!" Jessica screams from the side of the house, running toward us adults and breaking through the membrane of our circle.

Hunter gulps her into his arms and marvels at all the quarters.

In the distraction, Kira is able to disappear inside, doubtlessly thankful to not be the center of unwanted attention any longer.

"What is that all about?" I ask Dana.

"I'm not sure. All I know is that I *need* to find out."

We both laugh and head inside, leaving the party to unfold while we get things straightened out for Easter dinner.

I HAD to buy a dinner table for the occasion. Dana was the one who picked it out. A long, acorn-colored table with leaves that help extend it so each and every Solace (and those who are Solace adjacent) can belly up to the table.

It is decorated to the gills with colorful eggs dyed by the children, easter grass, and a centerpiece of a family of stuffed bunnies.

Dinner is a far cry from the dinners I had at holidays when I was kid. If I was lucky, it was me, Mom, and Dad. Most of the time it was just me and Mom.

Those were special celebrations. Although I know she always wished she was able to give me more.

My eyes linger on the mothers of the group. On Harley spoon-feeding some mashed potatoes into Tana's mouth, on Gillian scolding Stella making a smiley face out of peas and carrots on her plate, on Amy trying to keep Jessica from choking on her milk from laughing too hard.

That's going to be Dana soon. And that baby will be mine.

I've been wishing my mother could see me now.

Really, though, all I wanted was for my mother to be a grandmother. Here. With me.

I feel Dana's hand on my neck midway through the meal, her fingers playing with the piece of hair she lovingly calls my ducktail.

She's been able to sense my emotions far longer than I've been able to sense hers. A conceit of the way we laid the groundwork for our relationship. Over the years, I've learned her well. And in just the past few months, I've learned her even better. Our connection is deeper than ever, both literally and figuratively.

I glance at her and immediately feel warmth spread through my chest. Dana is beautiful. Every day. Every moment. But this moment somehow more than ever. Her lips bathed in coral lipstick, blonde waves tied into a messy bun, her pastel yellow dress showing off her pale collarbone. My eyes drift slightly lower to her belly. It's more obvious when she's sitting.

I wish my mom were here.

"I think we–" I look at the table without seeing. "Need more rolls, huh?" I push myself out of my chair and scurry into the kitchen before I can shed a tear.

Once in the kitchen, I lean over the sink and look out the window at the backyard. Perfect spot for a tire swing on one of the trees. Mom used to always say she wished she could make me a tire swing. Apartment living wasn't really conducive to customization.

"Why'd you have to go?" I whisper, blinking my eyes shut to release a single tear.

"Honey–"

I whip around to find Dana in the doorway. She holds up a basket from the table. "You're going to need this if you're going to get more rolls."

"Ah. Right." I slouch slightly and pull at the collar of my button down. Not used to wearing these things. "Thanks. I'll just be a minute."

I turn back around to the sink. Maybe a good splash of cold water on my face will do the trick.

Dana comes up behind me and wraps her arms around my waist. She leans her face against my back.

I sigh.

She draws away slightly. "I'll leave you alone if you want me to, but..."

I grab her hand. "No, no. Stay right there."

We remain locked in this embrace for a long time. Dana doesn't have to ask the question. She knows what's going on.

I say it anyway. "I miss my mom."

"I know, baby. I know. I miss her too."

I half-smile. "I wish you could have met her."

Dana nestles her head against my shoulder. "If you're anything like her, she must have been amazing."

She doesn't talk about her mother nearly as much as I talk about my own. Maybe it will come with time. I know the fondness isn't there in the same way. My mother was taken from me, hers chose to go. My mother can't be in our child's life. Hers chooses not to be. "It's not fair," I say, although I say it more for Dana than for me.

Dana pauses. "Not fair at all."

From the other room, there is a roar of laughter. The whole table seems to erupt in happiness. Children to adults, whatever just happened is funny beyond belief. I'm only a little sorry to have missed it.

Because here in the kitchen, Dana and I look at each other and smile. That's our future waiting for us. Our mothers might not be here, but we have plenty of loved ones to gather around the table, eat our food, celebrate our lives with us.

Everywhere we look is love.

I have Dana to thank for that.

I take her hand, stroking the friendship bracelet on her wrist. It's faded a bit over her time wearing it. She's never taken it off, not for a second. The threads will one day become bare and it will fall off and I'll have to make her another.

And the ring on her finger. A reminder that I still have one more step to take until our forever is signed, sealed, and delivered.

Dana settles her head against my chest. "I love you."

I pull her close and kiss her forehead. "I love you more."

"Don't you dare fight me on this. I definitely love you more. I'm having your baby, aren't I?"

"That's true, but unfair. I could never give you a gift like that. You'll have to take me at my word." I cup her cheek. "I love you more than anyone has ever loved anybody."

Dana doesn't fight back. And we both remain contented that the world has never seen a love quite like ours.

27

DANA

I wait for the mail truck to pull down the street before I go collect the mail. This daily habit that has been pedestrian most of my life has now become a daunting task. Comparable to the Twelve Labors of Hercules in what it takes me to get out to the mailbox.

I shiver to think at how much more effortful it will be once I'm later in my pregnancy and toting around quite a bit more weight on my front. For now, though, the fourth month pregnant belly I'm sporting doesn't get much in the way.

It's definitely undeniable now. My stomach pooches out just enough that no matter what I wear, there's a slight curve. I like walking around the world making it known that I'm going to be a mother. I don't know, something about it is that much more real when people can see it and it's not so much a secret.

Not to mention, we've made it through that tumultuous first trimester where you constantly wonder if you should have told so many people in case something goes wrong.

Four months, though. Four months looks and feels good on me.

Anyway, the mail.

I open the metal box and pull out a stack of letters and flyers. Some days, I don't even think mail should be allowed to exist when there are so many ads in your face all the time.

I shuffle through the stack. Bill, ad, ad, dental cleaning postcard.

I spy Drew's Tesla pulling down the street. Our street. He pulls up to where I stand on the sidewalk and hops out. "Hey, beautiful." He greets me with a kiss to the cheek that makes my insides tighten wondrously.

"Hey."

"How are you doing?"

Drew is home early from work for a very, very special occasion. "I'm great," I say with a smile, taking his hand. "Let me grab my purse and we can head out."

"Sounds good. I'll wait here."

I start down the walk.

"D!"

"What?"

"You look amazing."

I glance down at the outfit I've picked; a springy blouse and sleek skirt that really accentuates my bump. "I don't think I've ever dressed up this much to lay on an examination table."

Drew snorts and leans back on the Tesla. "You know that's not why you're dressed up."

I grin. When Drew told me last night he was going to take me out for a nice dinner after the appointment, I didn't think anything of it until he told me the place he chose was a very fancy fine dining establishment in Santa Monica. I had to dress the part. "I know, just giving you shit."

"Wouldn't have it any other way."

I head back inside quickly, dropping the mail into the mail slot on the counter to be sorted later. Today is my sixteen week checkup for the baby. I can't help the celebration that is getting to know how my little one is doing.

WE WERE lucky to be able to get an ultrasound with radiology scheduled for just after the appointment with my OB. Sure, I love having my blood drawn and giving urine samples as much as the next person, but the ultrasound is what we have both been really looking forward to.

"How've you been feeling, mama? Better now that you're out of the first, huh?" the young, springy-haired technician asks. She speaks as if she's been in my shoes.

"*Much*," I say as I shuffle back on the table and roll my skirt down over my belly for her before laying back.

"Here, honey," she says, pulling a stool up for Drew. "You don't need to stand there like Slender Man."

Drew laughs, an embarrassed flush on his face.

"He never knows what to do with himself during these things," I say, holding out my hand to him.

Drew takes it. "Listen, I've already imposed on your womb, I don't want to be an imposition elsewhere."

The technician giggles now. "Sounds like you've found a keeper."

"Definitely," I say.

"Cold." She squeezes the clear gel on my stomach. "So, when's the big day?"

I smile sheepishly. "Oh, the ring isn't–we're not–"

"Engaged to be engaged."

I throw Drew a look. That's the first time he's put it like

that. Sure, it was always implied. But we have been using the word "promise" to describe it. Not *engaged to be engaged*.

"Oh, noncommittal, hm?" The technician raises her eyebrow.

"No, nothing like that," Drew says. "Just prudent, I guess."

I squeeze his hand. He doesn't have to make excuses to people committed to misunderstanding our situation. "I'm in no rush."

He smiles gratefully, but the corners of his eyes look sad. As if he doesn't trust my confidence in him. Or something else I can't quite pin down.

The technician shrugs. "Well, at least he has good taste."

Before Drew can qualify it, say he had nothing to do with it, I say, "I think so too."

Drew relaxes beside me.

"Now, let's take a look at your bundle of joy, huh?"

The technician starts to spread the gel across my stomach with her wand, watching her screen as she does so. I wriggle my toes nervously, alternately observing her and then checking in with Drew for support.

The sound of the heartbeat cuts through the silence, a beautiful pounding.

"There's that heartbeat. Strong."

"That's what the doctor said last time," Drew murmurs.

He remembers everything when it comes to the baby. Not going to be one of those dads that forgets how old his child is (I only excuse my dad when he forgets because he had five of us). Drew might be even more on top of it than I am. He's already making sure there's a spot for our baby at his office daycare so I can eventually go back to counseling.

"Take a look."

The technician turns the screen and shows us the grainy black and white image. There's a baby in there alright. And it actually *looks* like one.

"There's the nose, mouth...And you can see right there a little hand. All fisted up. See?"

Drew and I both stare at the screen with rapt attention.

"Now, that baby looks very cozy," she coos.

"Aw, man." Drew pinches his nose bridge. "Not again."

The technician grabs a box of tissues and hands them to Drew. "Just to be safe."

"Thanks."

I pull his hand to my mouth and kiss his knuckles. If there's one thing I love more than seeing my baby on the monitor, it's seeing Drew see our baby.

"Now, did you want to know the gender?"

"What? I thought that was a twenty-week thing," Drew says urgently. "Not a—not a sixteen-week thing."

The technician turns the screen and shrugs. "We've got better tech now. And I can already tell what it is."

"Does that mean it's a boy?" I ask.

"I'm not saying unless you want to know," she replies with a sneaky smile.

I sigh and rest my head back on the table, looking up at the ceiling. We haven't talked about this yet. Didn't really anticipate that we'd be offered the gender already.

"What do you think, D?" Drew strokes the back of my hand with his thumb.

"I don't know. Do you want to know?"

"I want to know if you want to know."

"That's so much pressure, Drew!"

"Sorry, I–" He runs his hand back through his hair.

The technician clears her throat. "How about I count to three and then you both say what you want?"

That sounds...almost right. "What if we don't agree?"

"You can take that to couple's therapy."

I gulp. "Fair enough. Sound good to you?"

Drew nods. "I'm ready when you are."

"Alright, in one–"

Drew stops her. "Wait. *On* one or–"

"It's never *on* one!" I hiss.

"Okay, okay, fine! Sorry I asked."

The technician begins again. "One..."

God, do I want to know? Am I ready to know what we're having?

"Two..."

I'm still adjusting to a baby at all. A perfect, genderless bundle of joy that doesn't need to be anything but healthy. Do I need to throw the gender in there right now?

"Three."

Go time.

"Surprise."

Drew and I look at each other as if we've just spoken from the same voice box. Then, relief.

"Surprise it is. I'll get your pictures printed and you can live in blissful ignorance until you change your mind or baby is ready to meet you."

28

———————

EPILOGUE

DANA

We walk hand in hand down the beach. We had some time to kill between our appointment and our dinner reservation. We've been basking in the glow of a good report from the doctor and the anticipation of our baby's birth. Already. I don't want to rush it, but leaving the gender as a surprise is going to make that day even more special.

"So, I got some good news at work today," Drew says as an ocean breeze dances through his hair.

"You've been with me for several hours now and are *just* telling me this?"

Drew runs his hand through his beard. "Listen, this afternoon was about you. I didn't want to dim that with my stuff."

"There's always room for your stuff, D."

"I know, I know. But when it comes to the baby–"

"Just tell me! What happened at work?"

"Right, right. Well. My project got the final sign off. We're producing a prototype starting next month."

I leap into the air. "Drew! How did you keep that in for so long?"

"I told you, I–"

I throw my arms around his neck and pull my lips into his, an eager congratulatory kiss. "That's amazing. I'm so proud of you."

"Oh, it's nothing."

"Stop that. It's something. It's everything."

"Not compared to what you're doing."

I start to step away, rolling my eyes. "Would you quit it with the–"

Drew grabs my hand and pulls me back just in time that I narrowly avoid a squall of rollerbladers. I spin right back into his chest. He locks his arms around my waist. "No, I won't quit it. What you're doing right now is the height of human accomplishment. You're growing a whole fucking human being!"

"With your help, let's not forget."

"Yeah, but a night in bed four months ago is nothing compared to–"

"You know something?" I say, cutting him short.

His forehead screws together, resetting. "What?"

"You should never have been scared to be a dad."

His eyes, two blue pools, widen. "Oh."

"Because you..." I run my hands up and down his biceps. The arms that will hold our baby, comfort them, tuck them into bed, never let them go. "You were made for it, D."

If it's possible, his eyes widen more. "Don't make me cry *again*." He already lost it once more when he looked at the ultrasound pictures, as if he hadn't just seen the live rendering of our baby.

"See! This is what I mean. Literally made to be a dad. You've got 'dad' written all over you from your flannel to your beard."

"What's dad-like about my beard?!"

I throw my head back in laughter and pull on his hand. "Come on, let's go see if we can sit down early. I'm starving."

WHEN WE WALK into the restaurant, I immediately know something is off. It's...empty. And not just "we're eating at five o'clock because I'm pregnant and starving" empty.

We're the *only* people here.

And everything is immaculate from the flower petals on the table to the light streaming in through the gauzy curtains.

"This is beautiful," I say softly.

Drew leads me by the hand to the table where we are then greeted by a server who pours us water and gives us the first course of our meal, glistening bruschetta with buxom tomatoes. I dive in before he's even a step away, starving, not even questioning that the food is already coming out and I haven't ordered anything.

"If we aren't going to find out the gender, we need to pick out names for both, huh?"

"S'pose so," I reply, mouth full.

"I have a few Ideas."

Swallow, wait to respond before getting another mouthful, you're a lady after all, Dana. "Let me guess, they all begin with 'D'."

"Well, if you're open to it."

"Yeah, might as well get our family circus started."

Drew clears his throat and pulls out his phone. "Okay, here goes."

"You have a list of names on your phone?"

"Doesn't everyone?"

I resist telling him once again he's going to be an amazing dad and stuff my face with more bruschetta.

"So, for girls I have Diana—"

"Too much like the princess."

"Destiny."

"Too much like the Child."

"Desdemona."

"Do I even need to tell you that names form Shakespeare are off the table?"

"Oh, come on! Those would all be so cute. And you could call her 'Mona'."

"Too much like—"

"I know what you're going to say. The Lisa. Fine." He grumbles to himself. "Then here are some boy names."

We go back and forth like this, me totally ribbing him for his choices, him trying to convince me that they're so utterly wonderful I'd be a fool. However, when he gets to Digby, I have to stop him.

"What if we didn't stick with 'D' names, huh? Where would we be with that?"

Drew sighs. "In order to be creative, we need constraints."

"We're naming a child here, Drew. Not writing a sonnet."

He concedes with a shrug and then glances out at the sprawling beach and ocean just beyond the open windows. So handsome in golden hour.

I wish I could meet the woman that made him. The man too. I'd give him a piece of my mind. However, the woman that made him so fine and rare...I think about her every day. "If it's a girl, we should name her after your mom."

Drew straightens up the slightest bit. "Seriously?"

"Of course. I think it's only right. If you're comfortable with that, that is."

He stares at me for a long moment. Maybe I upset him. The last thing I want to do on a beautiful day like today is bring up his grief. But then, he smiles. "This is why you're so special, Dana."

"Oh, please." I pat off my lips with my napkin.

"Seriously, you're the most remarkable woman in the world."

I look down at the table, smiling through my bashfulness. "You're being sappy."

"You're damn right, I am. You're the mother of my child. The woman I love. I've got a right to be sappy, don't you think?"

Before I can respond, Drew gets out of his seat. I'm about to ask him where he's going, but then he lowers to the floor. On one knee.

"Oh, my god," I say. I grip the table, heart heaving itself into my mouth.

If there was any sliver of doubt about this being a proposal, it's quickly dashed away when he pulls a ring box out of his pocket. "Dana, as long as I've known you, you've been a light in my life." He clears his throat a bit, trying to hold back an onslaught of emotion. "I was alone in the world. Until you took me into your heart. Invited me into your family."

Out of the corner of my eye, there is movement. My dad enters followed by my sisters, followed by the men they love, and all three of my nieces.

I gape at them. "You're here..."

Dad blows me a kiss.

"I might not be a Solace, but you damn sure made me

feel like one," Drew says. "And to me that means walking through life with hope, knowing there will be people there to catch you when you fall, no matter what happens. People to clean your wounds. People who know you're human. And love you for it."

Now I'm the one crying.

"I only ever felt that with my mom. So, when I felt that with you, I knew I would love you forever. No matter if I could have you. Dana Solace would always live in my heart."

I touch my chest. I've never felt so surrounded by love in my life. All eyes on me. Ready and eager for my happiness.

"I considered myself the luckiest man in the world to have you as my friend. And I now consider myself even luckier because now you're my girlfriend."

"Engaged to be engaged," I tease through tears.

"You caught that, huh?" He grins. "Nothing gets past you."

We stare into each other's eyes for a long moment.

"Dana Solace is having my baby," he says, voice so fraught with ardor it's only a murmur. "And the only thing that could make me even luckier is if she's my wife. So..."

He opens the box. It's empty.

"I need that, actually," he says with a cheeky smile.

I laugh, let him take the ring off my finger and put it in the box. I had told him it would be foolish to get me a ring when his mother's is so beautiful. It would honor me to wear a piece of her the rest of my life in just this way. I'd rather him save that money for something else. Our future home or maybe a new car for once the baby arrives.

I have all the jewelry I need.

"I promise, Kent, I'm not a cheapskate," Drew says.

My dad laughs.

"D, will you marry me?"

"Yes, of course I'll marry you," I say, bursting at the seams. As soon as the ring is back on my finger and my family is celebrating, I throw myself into Drew's arms, kissing him on every square inch of his face. "I knew something was going on!"

"I'll never be able to surprise you, will I?"

On the contrary, Drew Young has surprised me over and over again. His willingness to fight for me. His commitment to being a father. The way he loves my family as if they're his own.

Because they are. My sisters are his. My father is his.

Drew fits right into a space that was always made for him.

I make the rounds to each of my family members, allowing them to fawn over me with kisses, hugs, and congratulations. Amy is already chiming in my ear about a double wedding which sounds like a nightmare.

I show them all the ultrasound pictures. The waterworks follow suit. I give Dad a copy I had printed especially for him and he puts it right into the breast pocket of his coat. "My first baby is having her first baby," he mutters with a gleam in his eye. "Nothing better than that."

The empty tables are for all of them. We all enjoy a lush, rich meal, beaming from ear to ear. While my family drinks champagne, the only thing Drew and I are drunk on is our happiness.

And I swear, toward the end of dinner, I feel the faintest fluttering in my belly. Not butterflies. A real one.

Life is just getting started.